Cynthia
of Bee Tree Hollow

GENEVIEVE FOX COLLECTION

By Genevieve Fox

First published in 1948

Cover design by Tina DeKam

Cover art by Embla Granqvist

Illustrations by Forrest W. Orr

This unabridged version has updated grammar and spelling.

© 2019 Jenny Phillips

www.thegoodandthebeautiful.com

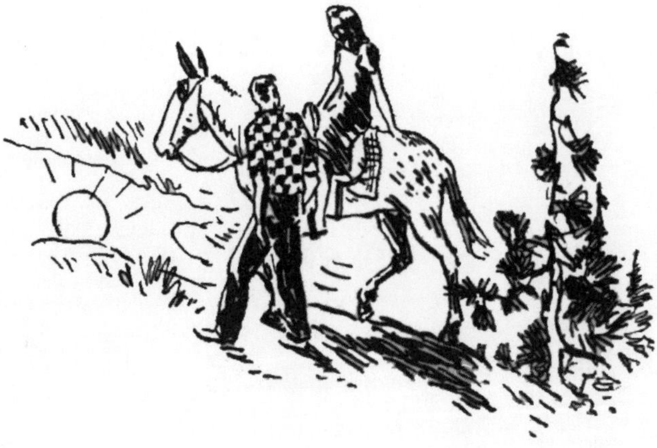

Contents

1. Cynthia is Worried 1
2. Cynthia Hides Pa's Gun 8
3. Surprises 14
4. The White Stake 21
5. "Miss Cynthia Bailey" 26
6. Cynthia Meets a Foreigner 31
7. The Pryingest Man 37
8. The Baileys Go to Town 41
9. "Where's That Money At?" 46
10. Cynthia Makes a Resolve 52
11. A Hole in the Earth 60
12. Dark Days 68
13. A New Teacher at Brightwater School 74
14. Granny Tries to Talk 79
15. Left Alone in the Hollow 83
16. "I Have to Find a Homeplace" 88
17. Cynthia Tears Down a House 94
18. A Big Time on Brightwater 100
19. A Week of Suspense 108
20. "Gee! You're Different!" 115
21. A Task for a Family of Giants 120
22. A Wonderful Feeling 124
23. Uncle Mose Acts Mysterious 129
24. The "Working" 133
25. Goodbye, Bee Tree Hollow 137
26. Welcome to Crabapple Creek 141
27. "You Don't Act Afraid" 147
28. Everything is Different 152

Chapter 1

Cynthia is Worried

To the flyer of the plane that droned over Brushy Mountain, the girl in a faded pink dress perched on the gray boulder looked like one more laurel bush in bloom. To the girl, the plane was like an enormous eagle hovering up there ready to pounce on a rabbit. Her blue eyes darkened as if a cloud had passed overhead. She jumped up and shook a small brown fist at the man in the sky. "Git away! Git away from here!" she yelled.

The plane kept on circling slowly above the mountainside for several minutes, then dropped lower and followed the threadlike stream which trickled down Bee Tree Hollow to Brightwater Creek. Not until it had disappeared beyond Sourwood Gap thirty miles away did the girl take her eyes off the machine. Even then, a frown still drew her eyebrows together.

That same plane or another like it had been here yesterday, flying up and down above the creek. She had seen it when she went to school and again at recess from the schoolyard. It seemed to be watching—watching for somebody or something. The boys said the flyer was a "revenooer" trying to find the Peterses' moonshine still. But that still was off over yonside Brushy, far away from here. And there certainly weren't any moonshiners along Brightwater.

She fitted herself again into her rain-hollowed seat in High Rock. It was, she liked to imagine, her throne, and all the lands below, her kingdom, walled in by a ridge of mountains. There was a gap in those mountains where the road wound through and down to the wide valley beyond. Yet often from here, they seemed to form a solid blue wall.

By leaning forward and peering through the branches of a hemlock, she could look down on the cabin at the head of this hollow where she lived, on the new, plank-sided house her brother Sam had built beyond, and even to the corner of the Hollow Road and the Creek Road where her sister Ella Martin and her husband, Joe, lived. A white belfry sticking out of the trees below Ella's place showed where the church house stood three miles away and where the cluster of buildings was which made up Brightwater village. It was fun to watch anyone riding or walking up the hollow and know that he couldn't see her on this hemlock-screened seat. Nobody could see her—nobody but that man in the sky.

Oh well, it was too pretty a day to be worrying about an old snooper. How the redbirds did sing! And that mockingbird was imitating them. Soon the girl's eyes were again the color of the haze that softened the hills. She began to sing:

> *Down in the valley,*
> *Valley so low,*
> *Hang your head over,*
> *Hear the winds blow.*
> *Hear the—*

She broke off. Someone was coming up through the woods on foot. It was a school day, and she wasn't supposed to be easing the time away like this. Alert as a squirrel, she watched the trail. Oh, it was just her Uncle Mose. He was a hunchback who lived by himself almost on top of the mountain. Must have been on one of his weekly trips to the Brightwater store, for his hunched shoulders were bowed lower than ever under a knobby-looking meal sack. Grabbing hold of a sapling which grew by the rock, she swung herself down into the woods below like a monkey.

"How you scared me, child! Seems like you drop out of the sky sometimes."

"I dropped out of that airplane." She laughed, then was sober again. "Uncle Mose, what's that man flying 'round here so much for?"

The gnome-like man lowered his sack to the ground and sat down on a rock to rest. "He's making a picture or a map—something like that—for the government. So folks say."

"For the government! Why, Uncle Mose, what would they do in Washington with a picture of Bee Tree Holler?"

"Laugh all you wants to, Cynthy, but that's what I heard. Only it ain't for Washington. It's fer the fellers that are building the big dam down on the river. I heard something else, too—something I sure hates to tell your Pa and Ma."

"Wha-at?"

"All the bottomland 'round here, clean up to the head of Bee Tree Holler, is going to be underwater when they get that dam done."

To the head of the hollow! That meant her own home would be under water. Terror was in her face for an instant. Then she burst out laughing. "Uncle Mose, do you know how far that dam is from here?"

He shook his head.

"Forty-five miles! That's what teacher told us."

"All the same, I'm right glad my cabin's yonside the mountain. It's a-going to be an almighty dam, Cynthy—that Lincoln Dam." He shook his head gloomily, got up, lifted the sack to his back again, and turned to go up the mountain. Then he asked, "Why ain't you in school, child?"

"Oh, Uncle Mose! I was ashamed to go. Couldn't do the 'rithmetic noways yesterday. I'm the stupidest one in the whole class 'most all the time." She was nearly in tears.

"All the more reason why you'd ought to go every day. Now I ain't starting home till you tells me you're a-going tomorrow, sure."

"I will, Uncle Mose."

The girl watched the little hunchback go scrambling up the steep trail and disappear into the woods. Her eyes had grown dark again. Now something cold and heavy as a stone lay in her stomach. If anybody but Uncle Mose had said those things about the dam, she wouldn't worry a mite. But he was wise—wiser than anyone else she knew. Like the Indians in the old days, who could put their ears to the ground and hear footsteps miles away before white men could hear a sound, the old man knew about things before other folks did. Of course, he picked up a lot of his news from the "foreign" women who had come from the level country and opened a store in Spruceville. They bought from him the "pretties" he carved out of pieces of wood and walnut shells and pinecones. And yet, Uncle Mose got hunches, too—hunches which had a way of coming true.

Cynthia climbed up on High Rock again. Everything was just the same. Turkey Hill below, with laurel and azaleas bursting in bloom all over it, still looked like one of Granny's prettiest bed "kivers." The redbirds and mockingbirds were as merry as they had been before Uncle Mose came along. Yet Cynthia Bailey did not hear the birds nor sense the beauty spread out at her feet. Her uncle's words were in her ears. The hollow below her seemed to turn into a lake of muddy water.

She had to go home, even if it meant a scolding for playing

hooky. This terrible story couldn't be kept to herself. Down she swung again. Tripping over tree roots and bruising her bare toes on sharp rocks in her hurry, in five minutes, she came panting to the gate. For an instant, the girl stood still and looked at her home as if she had never seen it before—at the silvery-gray cabin with its yellow limestone chimney and wide porch, the little old log springhouse, the garden with the roses budding, the two holly trees on either side of the door. Why, she had never before noticed how beautiful it was!

Her father and mother sat comfortably on the porch. Pa, with his chair tilted back against the wall and his battered hat tipped forward over his eyes, was smoking his pipe. Ma shucked beans into her blue-and-white checked apron and hummed a hymn tune softly to herself. Granny, as usual, was active as a spider. She stood poking sticks into the fire under the great iron wash kettle behind the springhouse, and punching and stirring rug rags about in a home-brewed dye.

"What ails you, Cynthy? You looks like you'd seed a hant." The old lady held in midair her dripping stick and stared at her youngest grandchild.

"Oh, Granny, I've just heard the most horrible news. You know that big dam they're starting to build down in the valley?"

"What about it?"

"Why, the water'll cover all our bottomland and wash away our house."

"Who's been a-filling you up with lies like that?" The cracked old voice rose till it could have been heard halfway down the hollow.

Pa Bailey brought his chair forward on all four legs with a bang. Ma stopped in the middle of the last verse of "Shall We Gather at the River?" The two half-grown hound pups, which had been sleeping on the sunny doorstone, leaped up and came rushing to meet Cynthia, barking hysterically.

"What you doing home from school this time of day?"

"You sick?"

Ignoring both parents' questions, the girl exploded her news again.

It was greeted with loud laughter from the two on the porch.

"Great guns and rattlesnakes, Cynthy, ain't you old enough to know a joke when you hears one?" asked her father.

"Uncle Mose wasn't joking."

"Joking or lying—one or the other. How could a little dam more'n forty miles from here push water way up into these hills? I've seen dams, and I've seen reservoys—one a mile long. They'd have to dig a ditch from here to the sea, child, and let the Atlantic Ocean loose to make a tide like that."

Color came back to the girl's cheeks.

Granny began to stir her rags again. Ma took up the hymn and the beans where she had left off. Pa tipped back against the wall. The puppies, convinced that all was well with their family, collapsed on the stone-paved walk just where they stood and where they were in everybody's way.

"If I was sure you'd made up this foolishness to get home early from school, I'd whip you," added Pa Bailey, who hadn't thought of that possibility before. He'd never whipped his youngest child—his "least child." And he knew and she knew that he never would. Yet his threats were often violent.

"I didn't make up a word of it. Uncle Mose told me what I've just been a-telling you."

Cynthia felt better. Uncle Mose must be wrong this time. Pa had seen dams—big ones. He knew what he was talking about. From sheer relief, she woke up the pups and began chasing them around and around in circles.

After supper, Enoch Bailey lifted down his banjo from the shelf over the fireplace in the front bedroom, tipped back in his chair on the porch, strummed the strings for a few minutes, cleared his throat, and began to sing old song-ballads he had learned as a boy. Presently, he was striking up the opening notes of a song he had composed himself.

> *Great-grandpap rode over the mountains*
> *In eighteen hundred and three,*
> *To find him a wilderness homeplace,*
> *Rode clear from the banks of the sea.*

There were eight stanzas. Pa sang all eight, ending exultantly with a ninth, which he made up as he went along:

> *The cabin still stands 'neath the mountain,*
> *The Baileys still live on the land,*
> *As safe from the floods and the tempests*
> *As if in the palm of God's hand.*

Cynthia sat on the doorsteps and listened while Bee Tree Hollow slowly became a pool of darkness, and the whippoorwills began to call from the edge of the woods. It seemed as if a quiet hand was laid on her troubled spirit. There had been Baileys here more than a hundred years ago. There would be Baileys here when a hundred more years were gone.

Yet, when she lay in bed, Uncle Mose's words began to repeat themselves maddeningly over and over in her ears—all the bottomland clean up to the head of Bee Tree Hollow under water. Under water. Under— What was that roaring sound? It was Brightwater Creek. No, it was the Bee Tree Branch. Here it came, a wall of swirling, foaming water. Oh, this was like the big flood she had long remembered. Run! Run! They would have to climb up on the mountain again. How could she ever carry all these blankets and her clothes and the cat? She was stumbling, falling, crying out.

"Cynthy! Wake up!" called Ma Bailey from the door. "You're having a nightmare."

Chapter 2

Cynthia Hides Pa's Gun

Next day at the Brightwater School, the boys and the girls did not play games. They didn't even throw rocks. Instead, they repeated things they had heard and watched the sky for an airplane to come flying back through Sourwood Gap.

Just the top of Brushy Mountain would be sticking up out of the water when that dam was done, Buddy Fuller, the storekeeper's son, announced. The man from the wholesale house had told his father so, and his pa was going to start looking for another store right away.

Hattie May Wheeler said the man from the wholesale was trying to scare Buddy's father. The water wouldn't come any nearer than lower Brightwater. Her uncle had talked to the first selectman of Spruceville, and he had it from a man who was working down there near the dam, and she "reckoned he'd oughter know."

Cynthia's best friend, Linda Wilson, was sure that her family would have to move. She didn't know about Bee Tree Hollow, but Squire Johnson at the county seat had told her folks that Brightwater Valley was sure to be all under water, and Squire ought to know.

"Oh, Linda! Your homeplace under water." There was a

catch in Cynthia's voice. The Wilson place was no cabin. It was a big, comfortable house two stories high, with tall chimneys and a wide porch across the front, upstairs and down. The best times in her whole life had been visits there. Playing games with Linda and her brother Paul before blazing fires indoors. Playing in summer under the great trees in the yard.

The two girls had been eating lunch together, but Cynthia couldn't finish hers. Ma's good, light bread stuck in her throat now.

Rumors ran like brush fires in a high wind up Brightwater Creek and up all its small branches. Every day Pa Bailey went down to the store for the latest news, and every day he came back with a different story. Yet all the stories were said to come straight from people "who oughter know what they was talking about."

When was the terrible day coming—the day when folks would have to move out? Nobody knew. Some said a man might show up at any time now and order them right off their own land. Others said the government would have to give thirty days' notice. It was the law. Mose was sure that a big dam like Lincoln Dam couldn't be built in less than two years. The president of Spruceville Bank told Matt Wilson that the head engineer told him that everyone would have time to harvest this year's crops. Yet Brightwater folks began to look anxiously down the creek every day for "foreigners," as they called anyone who lived outside their mountains.

Talk at Fuller's store grew louder and hotter. Men began to threaten to shoot any stranger at sight. After one of these heated sessions, Enoch Bailey came home with little flames in his eyes. He went straight to the kitchen and grabbed his gun from the shelf above the stove, knocking over a bucket of skimmed milk and stepping on the cat in his haste. He gave it a good cleaning and reloaded it. Grimly, he propped the rifle against the house beside the door.

Cynthia's eyebrows drew together into an anxious frown. How could Pa think that anything but trouble would ever come from pointing a gun at a man from the government? Hadn't Link Peters tried that with a "revenooer" who was looking for his moonshine still, and wasn't Link in jail? Times had changed. The law could reach the head of every little hollow now.

Two members of the Bailey family were not worried. One was Ella Martin, the oldest Bailey daughter, who lived with her husband, Joe, in the last house on the Hollow Road. She said she'd be "darned glad to get out of this hole." Maybe Joe could get a job down at the dam, and maybe they could live in one of those brand-new houses the government was building for the workers.

"You and Joe don't put down no more roots than a bean vine," her father told her disgustedly.

Ella and Joe were not like the rest of them. They had "seen the world"—seen it from three coal-mining towns and two cotton-mill villages. They hated Bee Tree Hollow and longed for movies, dances, stores, and near neighbors. Joe's laziness was the only thing that kept them from living in town all the time. "If anybody comes along and offers you cash-money for this old place, grab it, Pa." That was Ella's advice.

Granny wasn't worrying either. She didn't believe a word of "all this fool talk." The old lady could remember wild stories people had told sixty years ago when the railroad began to buy up land in this country. Her pappy had been certain the tracks were going right through his cornfield, and then the road didn't come within ten miles of his place.

One night the family at the head of the hollow woke from a deep sleep to hear a voice yelling, "Git up! Git up, everybody! Quick! Quick!"

It was past midnight. Pa Bailey leaped from bed and ran out of the house to see if the chimney was on fire or the barn in flames. "It's the dam!" cried Ma Bailey. "It's the big tide coming."

Granny was scared, too. Half asleep, she was back in her girlhood, reliving the War between the States. She thought the Yankees were coming again.

"Git up! Git up! The end of the world's coming." The cry was nearer now. They recognized that shrill voice and burst out laughing. It was Billy Wheeler. Billy had a man's body, but his mind had never grown up. All week he had been listening to the men gossiping in the store until something inside him had exploded.

Pa Bailey brought him into the house. "Sit down and catch your breath," he ordered. Ma lighted all the lamps, then brought him buttermilk and cookies. "You've got kinda mixed up, Bud," Pa told him. "The world ain't a-coming to an end for another year."

"Is that a fact?" asked Billy solemnly.

"Sure is."

The cookies, which he ate ravenously, and the talk quieted him. In a few minutes, he was grinning and telling about the coon his dog had treed night before last. Then Pa lit his lantern, backed One-eye, the half-blind mule, out of his stable, and took Billy home behind him on the saddle.

That gun kept bothering Cynthia. Night and day it stood there beside the kitchen door. Pa was just bluffing, she told herself. Yet a terrifying picture grew more and more vivid in her imagination, a picture of what might happen. A stranger would walk right up on the porch and say the Baileys had to move. Pa would see red and grab the gun. He wouldn't know what he was doing till the stranger fell. Then the sheriff would come with a pair of handcuffs.

She had to do something. But what? Hide the gun and keep it hidden until her father had time to cool off. That was what she must do. It was a simple plan. The hard part was carrying it out. Always somebody seemed to be near the kitchen door—coming in or going out or sitting on the porch or puttering with the flowers in the yard.

A rainy Sunday brought Cynthia her opportunity. The whole family, instead of sitting in the kitchen, as usual, were in the big front room where Granny slept, and where she had her loom and quilting frame. Granny and Ma knitted. Pa snoozed over the *Weekly Spruceville Record.* The girl waited till the paper dropped from his hand. She listened till his snoring was regular and deep. Then, murmuring something to herself about letting Goldie, the cat, out, she let herself out at the same time. Slowly she pulled the door to, trying to make no sound. Bang! The wind jerked it out of her hand. The pups woke up and began to whine and scratch to follow her. That meant opening the door again before they set up a din and spoiled everything. Pa Bailey snorted, then slept again.

A quick snatch! A dash across the yard to the barn! Ah, now she would slip the gun into that niche in back of the mule's stall. It would not be discovered for months. Pa would think somebody had stolen it. He would make an awful row, but he couldn't do any shooting, no matter how many foreigners came around. For the first time since leaving the house, she breathed naturally. Then the barn door opened.

"Cynthy Jane Bailey!" Pa roared. "You fetch that gun to me, and you fetch it quick!"

She fetched it.

"What you think you're doing with my gun?"

"I—I was hiding it."

"Hiding it?"

"I'm—I'm—" How could she explain with her father staring at her as if he thought she had suddenly gone crazy and would have to be shut up? "I'm scared, scared you'll kill somebody and get yourself hanged. You keep that little old gun too handy."

Enoch Bailey snatched his property from her hand and strode out of the barn without another word.

Cynthia climbed into the haymow and threw herself down on the sweet-smelling hay. It seemed best to stay away from the house for a long time.

Outside the kitchen door, the gun stood again, ready for action.

Chapter 3

Surprises

"He's coming! Hide quick, everybody!" called Linda Wilson in a loud whisper.

The big shady yard of the Wilson place had been full of chattering young folks. Suddenly it was empty. Cynthia crouched behind the rain barrel, holding the skirt of her blue dress close against her body. Hattie May Wheeler took to cover in the honeysuckle bushes. The two older Wheeler boys pressed themselves against the wide trunks of two oak trees. Buddy Fuller went up the trunk of a pine like a cat and straddled a high branch. Sally and Sue, the Wilson twins, aged seven, sat on the porch steps and giggled—and giggled—and giggled.

Linda did her best to make up for their suspicious behavior. "Hi, Paul!" she sang out, putting on an elaborately unconcerned air.

A tall boy with bright dark eyes ran through the gate, letting it slam behind him. "Lookit! Lookit!" he called excitedly, holding up a long string of trout.

At that moment, his mother's broad figure appeared through the kitchen door. She carried straight in front of her an enormous ham on the biggest platter she owned.

"Thought you wanted me to catch fish for dinner, Ma." Now he saw the long table decorated with flowers and colored paper napkins and set up for eleven. "Wha—What's going on?"

"Ka-choo!" Buddy couldn't hold that sneeze a second longer.

"Hey! Who's up there?"

At once, the bushes and trees came to life. "Happy birthday, Paul! Happy birthday!" A chorus of voices greeted him.

So this was it. This was why he had been fairly urged to go up North Branch fishing.

Cling-clang, cling-cla-ang. It was the big dinner bell ringing from the belfry on top of the house. Linda pulled the rope till the notes went pealing up and down Brightwater Creek and echoed from the sides of Turkey Hill.

With the echoes, shouts came down out of the woods. Everybody looked up to the hillside. Two boys had emerged into the clearing. They began scrambling down the steep path.

"Why, it's Billy and Steve!" Paul waved both arms. "Gee whiz! How many are coming, anyhow?"

Billy and Steve Jenkins were his cousins who lived on the other side of Turkey Hill at Jenkins Cove. It was twenty miles to and from their homeplace by the road, but only five miles if one climbed straight up into the air on one side and slipped and slid down the other. The two barefooted, long-legged boys greeted the yard full of young people with quick, bashful "howdies," and slyly placed a bulky, newspaper-wrapped package on the table.

"Cousin—Lou—and—Cousin—Willa May—are a-coming," panted out the twins, dashing up from the creek where they had been watching the road.

Paul made for the house. No girl cousins were going to catch him in muddy, fishy overalls and barefoot.

The faces of the girls were two wide smiles as they rode into the yard, one behind the other, on a mule. Not often at this busy time of year did they get a chance to ride Billy the seven miles from Shady Valley to visit the Brightwater cousins.

Almost as soon as the girls were off the mule, Paul was in the yard again. He was colorful as his mother's garden in bright blue cotton slacks and a plaid sports shirt.

"Everybody eat 'fore the victuals get cold," commanded Mrs. Wilson. "Paul, you set at that end, and Linda up here, and the rest where you please."

Cynthia looked up and down the table. She was glad now that she had gotten up early and washed her hair and pressed her blue dress. Those pretty cousins from Shady Valley looked as if they'd walked straight out of the mail-order catalog in new dresses. Linda was lovely to see in her white dress. But then, it didn't make much difference what a girl wore if she were tall and slender and dark, Cynthia thought enviously. Too bad she couldn't really see herself—how sunbeams seemed always to be caught in her brown hair, and how her blue eyes looked as if lights were turned on behind them when she smiled.

The young folks were left to eat and chatter by themselves. Now their happy voices and their laughter drowned out the whistles of the redbirds overhead and the rushing sound of Brightwater Creek below. Parties were rare for all of them, and they were making the most of this one. The Wilsons, with their acres of rich bottomland, lived better than their neighbors up in the little hollows and on the hillsides. Mrs. Wilson had fairly outdone herself and prepared a feast. "We'll give them a big time today," she told her husband. "The good Lord only knows where they'll be next year."

The eleven young people ate like hounds. The huge ham was sliced down to the bone. The white-domed, candle-lit birthday cake was reduced to crumbling ruins. Cream-drenched strawberries seemed to melt in the dishes, and the tall pitchers of lemonade had to be filled over and over.

Paul began unwrapping the packages in front of his place.

They were all home-grown or homemade, except the fly-specked box of candy Buddy brought from his father's store. The large package toted over Turkey Hill by the Jenkins boys proved to be wild honey.

"We found a bee tree yesterday," they explained. Cynthia's gift was a pair of sports socks she had been knitting for months, in Paul's favorite colors—tan with orange stripes.

The trees in the Wilson yard had been looking down on family gatherings for a hundred years, yet never on a merrier one than they saw today, and never had more laughter gone ringing up through their branches. There were stunts and games. The boys put on tree-climbing and rock-throwing contests, which the girls jeered and cheered. Boys and girls played a noisy and lawless game of baseball. Then the boys raced each other to the swimming hole. Their splashings and whoopings could be heard clear back in the yard, where the girls lolled on the pine needles and talked. They talked easily and a little breathlessly, as if they had much to tell each other before the boys came back.

There was just one thing wrong with that May afternoon. The sun seemed to race down the sky toward Brushy Mountain. And nearly everyone must go home early. The two sets of cousins had long trips to take before dark. Cynthia had promised to cook supper and milk Jumping Jane because Ma and Granny were canning strawberries today. The Wheelers were always needed at home; there was so much work to do in the mill and on the farm, and so many young Wheelers to look after.

"Before anybody goes home," announced Paul, when they were back in the yard, "I want you to print your initials here." He pointed to the wooden seat under one of the pine trees. "Then I'll carve them out with my knife and cut the date on, too."

One by one the guests took a pencil and knelt or squatted down to inscribe their letters in the silver-colored wood of the old seat. Paul looked it over to make sure no initials were missing. "There!" he said, "I'm going to keep that old bench always. And if we have to leave here, I'm going to take it with me."

Cynthia felt as if a cold wind had blown suddenly down-creek. Yet the May breeze was soft like the touch of a feather. She shivered at the thought of this cool green room with its pine-needle floor being under water.

"Wait till the rest are gone, Cynthia, and I'll walk a piece with you," whispered Paul.

By four o'clock they were going up-creek together, Cynthia on One-eye and Paul walking alongside. His stride kept up easily with the lazy mule's pace. Neither spoke for a few minutes.

The girl found it harder to talk with Paul than she used to when he and Linda and she all went up to the Brightwater School together. He was in Spruceville High now, and in his second year. More and more he dressed and acted like a town boy. He was talking all the time more like a town boy. She had begun to feel conscious of her own mountain speech when she was with him, and that she was two years younger than he, and small for her age.

"Haven't had so much fun in ages," he told her.

"Nor I."

"And we're all going to keep on having fun together. No dam is going to stop us." His voice was almost angry. The determination in it comforted Cynthia.

"Want to know what present I liked best?" he asked.

"Sure do."

"The socks you knit. They're fine-pretty."

Her smile was beautiful.

They drew near an unpainted building with packaged groceries and fly-specked soft drink signs in the window. The girl began to talk faster. She expected Paul would leave her there at the store, for she knew he had an errand to do for his mother. He did not stop but kept right on—by the Wheelers' mill, by the box of a church house which stood high on a knoll in front of a white-fenced graveyard, and on past the unpainted one-room schoolhouse.

Just before they came to Brightwater Four Corners, he reached into the patch pocket of his shirt, pulled out a newspaper clipping, and handed it to her with a self-conscious grin. It was from the *Spruceville Record*.

"'Brightwater Boy Breaks Tie Score,'" she read. "'Home Run Wins Game for Spruceville High.' Oh, Paul! That's you! In the newspaper! In the headlines, too."

The grin widened as he saw her delight.

"You always was the best player 'round here. Now you're the best in Spruceville."

"Sa-ay, why can't you come down some Saturday and see a game?"

She looked at him as if he had proposed a lovely but impossible adventure. It was a long ride by mule to the county seat. On rare occasions, the Baileys went jolting down there in a wagon behind One-eye and Sam's mule, Gideon, but they always had to start home again before midafternoon.

Now they were at the Four Corners where Brightwater Road crossed another which led in one direction up North Branch and in the other up Bee Tree Hollow. Here Cynthia had to turn off.

"We-ell," said Paul, "reckon I have to go back."

"Goodbye."

"Goodbye. See you soon." He went running down the creek, whistling as he ran.

The girl reined the mule onto the deep-rutted road with grass in the middle. She sang softly to herself. Just beyond the corner was the cabin where her sister Ella lived.

"Howdy, Cynthy," she called from the porch. "Did you have a big time?"

"Sure did. I'll be down tomorrow and tell you about it. Go 'long, One-eye."

Ella's news couldn't be kept till tomorrow. "Uncle Mose came by a little while ago. He said surveyors was yonside Brushy this morning, a-traipsing all over. Reckon they're somewhere up in the holler now."

"What's surveyors?"

"They're the guys that's going 'round looking through little spyglasses and measuring off the land for the dam."

Cynthia stopped to hear no more. "Go on, One-eye! We have to get home quick!"

Chapter 4

The White Stake

"All right, lie there, you hateful, ornery old critter you!" Cynthia shook her fist at One-eye's face and picked herself up out of the dirt. The mule had done what he often did when anyone tried to hurry him—lain down in the middle of the road, rolled his rider off, and refused to move.

The girl started on. She ran the rest of the way, slowing down only now and then to ease her panting.

"Yoo-hoo!" she called from the gate. Her voice broke through the heavy stillness. The Bailey place was as deserted as the church house on a weekday. No sound came from the house or the barn. Not even a pup barked. Her eyes sought the door from the kitchen onto the porch. Then all the warm color left her cheeks. The gun was gone.

"Ma! Granny!" No one was in the house. The kitchen was fragrant with strawberries. On the wood stove sat a wash boiler. The water in it had stopped boiling. The fire under it was low.

Outside again, her eyes searched the garden, the corn patch, the hillside pasture. A spot of blue was moving just above the pasture gate. It was Granny's sunbonnet. The girl started after the bonnet as if it were a banner. Scrambling over the rail fence, she took a shortcut through the corn. Oh dear! Oh dear! Jumping Jane must have broken out again. Row after row of the pale green plants were eaten off or trampled down.

"Granny," she panted as soon as she was within calling distance, "where is everybody?"

"Yonder!" The old lady pointed a trembling finger up the hill. "Low-down, sneaking furriners come down over Brushy and tore down the fence and let Jumping Jane and the spotted calf into—"

Cynthia waited to hear no more. She saw now that she was the rear guard of a short procession. Several rods ahead of Granny, Ma Bailey hurried up through the clearing, and a little way beyond her stood Pa, gun in hand, with the pups yelping and growling at his heels. He was facing a tall man in khaki.

The tall man was bent over a three-legged thing. What was it? A camera? No. It was a spyglass on legs. As the girl watched, he straightened up and waved some kind of signal toward the woods above him. There was another khaki-colored figure up there. She looked from one to the other fearfully, as she might at two strange animals.

Now her father's voice rose above the barking of the dogs. He was ordering the foreigner off his land and brandishing that gun. The tall man began to talk. His voice was calm and too low-pitched to carry far. He did not have a chance to say much before Enoch Bailey broke in again.

"Git off my land!" he commanded.

Cynthia's heart was up in her head, pounding so hard she couldn't think anymore. It was happening—just what she had pictured for weeks: a man from the dam, her father getting angrier and angrier, his gun all ready. She tried to run up an almost straight pitch but had to slow down. She shouted to her father, but he did not hear her.

The two men talking together saw something blue fly through the air and land between them. "Don't shoot him, Pa!" a girl's voice shrieked.

"You keep out of this, Cynthy!"

"Thanks, little girl." The young man sounded amused instead of grateful. "There isn't going to be any shooting. I was just telling your father that I really have a right to be here. I'm surveying for the Lincoln Dam, and—" He broke off suddenly. Nobody could talk with a girl looking at him like that. Her eyes were two blazing fires above scarlet cheeks.

"You didn't have no right to knock down our fences and let the cow out to tromp down our corn, nohow."

"Did I do that, little girl? I should have thought about cows being in here. I was raised on a farm myself."

"I'm not a little girl, and your slick talk won't make that corn grow again." Angry as she was, Cynthia had to admit to herself that he sounded sorry and that his hazel eyes were kind.

The tall man turned to Enoch Bailey as if dismissing her. "Tell you what, Mister, figure out how much you've lost on that corn, and take it up with the land appraiser when he comes. He'll see that you're paid."

"The wha-a-at?"

"A man will be coming around in a few weeks to ask you questions about the value of your land and buildings."

"He will, will he? I'll be waiting for him."

"Now, if I were you, I'd take this thing easy, Mister, er—"

"Bailey's my name."

"By the way, I haven't introduced myself. I'm Jim Holliday."

"I don't care who you are. Just take yourself off my land."

"Okay. We're done on this side of the mountain."

Folding up his instrument and shouldering it, he moved up the path that led over Brushy. Just before he came to the woods, Jim Holliday stopped under the big hickory tree. Now what was he doing? It sounded as if he were pounding something under the tree. In a few moments, he and his companion vanished into the woods.

Ma and Granny, who had both kept in the background, came up now and began to ask questions. "What's he drove into the ground up thar under the tree?" demanded the old lady.

They climbed the steep slope. From among the black shells of last year's nuts gleamed a white stake. All four stared at it for a moment, then Pa Bailey, swearing under his breath, grabbed the offensive thing. It was too firmly driven in to pull up by hand.

"I'll git my crowbar and pull that thing right out."

"What's it mean—that stick? Are they a-going to lay railroad tracks right over Brushy?" Again she was mixing up past memories with present happenings.

"Means somebody turned a fool loose in here, that's all."

Cynthia looked into her father's face to see what she could read in it. The white stakes men were driving into the hillsides were high-water marks. So folks were saying. Would all the hollow and half the mountainside pasture be under water? Would the old hickory tree stand on the edge of a lake and drop its nuts into watery depths instead of where she could gather them? Was her father thinking these things and just pretending before the women-folks that the man sent out to survey the land for the great dam didn't know his business?

Back down to the house trailed the procession of four people and two dogs. The people were silent and sagged a little as they walked. Even the puppies were quiet.

Enoch Bailey went directly to the barn, but he did not get the crowbar. Instead, he sat in the doorway and stared down the hollow for a long time. The women rushed to the kitchen, suddenly remembering their canning. In silence, they began rebuilding the fire under the boiler and clearing up the unwashed dishes. The girl sat down on the stone seat in the springhouse for a moment to calm herself. Usually, she loved to rest by the pool of water and hear the spring talk softly as it trickled down into the branch. Now even the talking spring sounded troubled.

Chapter 5

"Miss Cynthia Bailey"

It was Saturday—and no ordinary Saturday for Cynthia Bailey. She was dashing from bedroom to kitchen, from kitchen to bedroom, outdoors and in again. She was heating water on the kitchen stove and washing her brown hair till it was full of bright glints. She was pulling basting threads out of the new dress Ma had helped her make. The dress was white with pink flowers all over it, and Cynthia's cheeks were as pink as the flowers, she was so excited.

No wonder. She was going to the square dance in the Spruceville Town Hall with Linda and Paul Wilson, and this was the first time she had ever been to a town dance. Paul was driving up to the Four Corners to meet her in the Wilson car. She was staying the night at the big house on Brightwater Creek.

Just to think of going to a Spruceville dance made her feel grown up. Yet she did wish she wasn't so small and childish-looking for her age. Hadn't that surveyor called her "little girl" and treated her like one, too? His patronizing manner rankled in her memory.

It was the prettiest time of day when she started to walk to the Four Corners. The sky above Brushy Mountain was soft pink pricked by a single bright star. It was the prettiest time in all the year, too—rhododendron time. Both sides of the road were banded with pink blossoms. And Cynthia—blue-eyed, pink-cheeked, her small-featured face framed by soft curls, in her pink and white dress—she was prettier than the sunset or the evening star or the flowers.

"Look at Cynthy! All dressed up!" Her brother Sam's children caught sight of her the moment she rounded the bend in the road and came on a run to meet her.

"Where you a-going?" demanded Dan, the oldest.

"What you all dressed up for?" asked the next oldest.

"Come and play with us," begged Ellie Lou, who was the youngest except for the baby.

"Grab Rosey! Don't let her jump on me," yelled Cynthia at the sight of their muddy-pawed hound, bounding to meet her.

All three gave chase, and children and dog became involved in a game of their own and forgot about Cynthia.

"Stop and rest yourself," called her brother, who sat on the porch smoking his pipe.

"Can't, Sam. Going to the dance down at Spruceville with Linda and Paul."

Mattie, Sam's wife, stopped in the midst of putting the baby to bed and came to the kitchen door. "Well, well, little Cynthy's going to town to a dance!" she exclaimed.

There was not another house till she came to the cabin just above the fork in the road. Here, the girl well knew she would have to stop for inspection.

"Where you a-going?" came the expected voice from the porch.

"You couldn't even guess, Ella. I'm going to town to a dance."

"For goodness sake, Cynthy, you ain't wearing sneakers to a dance, are you?" Ella was looking her sister over from the top of her head to her feet.

"Course I'm not. Got my good ones here in a poke." She held up a brown paper bag.

"You reckon them Spruceville High boys will ask me to dance with them?"

"Well, I don't know, Cynthy. You look like such a little kid. Nobody would take you for fourteen." Ella was never anything but frank with her family.

Younger sister winced. "They wouldn't?"

"How'd you like to have me fix you up a bit? Bet I can make you look sixteen and so pretty the town guys will fall over each other to dance with you."

"O-oh Ella! Reckon you could?"

"Come on in."

Older sister led the way to a cluttered bedroom, sat Cynthia down in front of a looking glass, and went to work on her. First, she refitted the new dress, pinning it, then sewing the seams with long hasty stitches, in contrast to the neat, fine seams Cynthia had sewn with pride.

"There, it don't look so much like a meal sack now," she exclaimed with satisfaction.

Next, she brushed the brown hair, which lay in natural curls on the girl's shoulders, high in an upswept hairdo. Pulling out a cheap makeup kit, she now began on her sister's face, darkening the delicately etched eyebrows, tinting her lips vividly and even reddening the already pink cheeks.

"You've got plenty of color now 'cause you're heated up, but you'll git washed-out looking without some rouge," Ella explained.

"Is that me?" the girl exclaimed when the "beautifying" job was complete.

"No. Meet Miss Cynthia Bailey from Spruceville. Now wait a minute." She burrowed around in her closet and brought out a pair of spike-heeled, patent leather pumps somewhat crackled with age. "See if you can wear them."

Cynthia of Bee Tree Hollow

Cynthia tried her best to force her feet into the pumps. It couldn't be done, and this was probably fortunate for her enjoyment of the dance.

"Child, you're ruining your feet going barefoot. That spreads them terrible," Ella told her.

Giving a last dab at Cynthia's hair, and a few pokes and pulls to the new dress, she sent her little sister off delighted, a little sister who was sure she could pass for a young lady. "You look pretty and right stylish now," she called after her.

> *"I got a girl at the head of the holler,*
> *Hey-ho, diddle dum dey!"*

sang out Paul as the girl came around the corner on light feet. He was waiting in the high-slung car the Wilsons had driven ever since Cynthia could remember, and he was all dressed up in tan slacks and a sports shirt as colorful as the flags of all nations.

"Well, well, Miss Cynthia Bailey!" The boy stared with his mouth open at the results of sister Ella's heavy-handed making-up. "You look almost as old as my Aunt Bess."

"That's the way I wants to look," she said firmly.

"You're too pretty to have your cheeks daubed up like that, and I like your hair down better, too."

Cynthia rubbed off onto her handkerchief a little of the hectic flush Ella had given her, but nothing could have induced her to change the grownup-looking hairdo.

On the wide porch, Mr. and Mrs. Wilson sat in their Sunday clothes waiting patiently. They liked a square dance perhaps even better than the young folks did. Besides, Mr. Wilson had no idea of letting Paul "take off down to the county seat with the car at night."

Over the railing of the balcony above, a white-clad figure leaned. "Hi, Cynthia!" The girl's voice was excited.

"Hi, Linda!"

By dusky dark they were on their way, driving through the cool, dim woods along lower Brightwater. In half an hour, they had turned onto a hard-surfaced black road. After that, it seemed no time at all before the houses began to draw closer and closer together. In another half hour, the road had turned into a main street. It was still a wonder to the Bee Tree Hollow girl how quickly one could go to town in a car.

Here was the big brick building where Paul went to high school. Next fall, Linda would go there, too. Will I ever get to high school? The girl asked the question silently and hopelessly. She could see herself going on at the Brightwater School or some other little school, trying and trying to pass arithmetic tests and always failing. In a year or two, she would be so old, she would feel ashamed to stay in school any longer with the little kids.

Chapter 6

Cynthia Meets a Foreigner

Here they were at the town hall. What a sight of cars! And what a sight of folks! Cynthia's cheeks grew redder than her makeup. She walked stiffly and self-consciously between the lines of men and boys on both sides of the walk and the town hall steps. They were staring hard at every girl, obviously deciding whether they wanted to dance with her or not.

"Don't guess I get to dance much," she told Linda when they were inside the hall. "Didn't see more'n three boys out there I know, and they're younger than me."

"Paul will look out for us. He's got to. Who you reckon the guys are, all dressed up with their coats on? They don't come from Spruceville nohow."

Discordant sounds arose above the din made by some fifty women and girls all talking—the scraping of Uncle Dan Collins' fiddle strings, the plink-plink of Billy Jones' guitar, and the plunkety-plunk of Mark Williams' banjo. The Spruceville Music Makers were tuning their instruments. Without warning, they struck up "Sourwood Mountain."

"Choose your partners," bellowed Uncle Dan.

In came the men and boys stomping, snickering, looking about for certain girls. Paul headed for Linda and Cynthia.

Who was that with him? One of the young men "all dressed up with their coats on." A foreigner, Cynthia decided. This man, though he was brown and muscular, looked well fed and almost soft beside the men and boys around him, who were as lean and rangy as their own hound dogs. His smile was readier, too, than the smile of a mountain man, and to wear a coat to a dance and get yourself all sweaty, that was just foolishness.

"Linda, Cynthia, this is Jim Holliday. Come on, Cynthia." Thus Paul introduced the stranger, turned him over to his sister, and asked Cynthia for a dance all in one breath.

Jim Holliday? The girl stared up into a pair of smiling hazel eyes. Yes. It was that surveyor! She hadn't recognized him at first in those clothes.

Paul took her arm and skipped with her across the floor to join the circle. Linda and the surveyor followed.

"Change partners!" called Uncle Dan presently, and Cynthia found herself locking arms with young Holliday. He stared, then grinned. "If it isn't the little girl who saved my life up on the mountain!" The dance separated them.

"Swing your corner lady!"

They were together again for a moment.

"I wasn't aiming to save you nohow. I just didn't want Pa to get into any trouble on account of you," she explained bluntly.

"Perhaps when you know me better, you'll decide I'm worth saving after all."

There was no chance to answer until he swung his "corner lady" again. "You live on the side of that mountain?" he asked.

"No, at the foot of it."

"Come to Spruceville often?"

"Once or twice a year."

"Is that all? May I have the next dance?"

"Reckon so," she told him over her shoulder, as Paul swung her.

When the call "Form a Ring" came again, Jim Holliday claimed her promptly.

"Is that old dam going to flood Bee Tree Hollow sure?" She fixed anxious eyes on his face, waiting for his answer.

"Can't tell you, not without studying my maps."

"Spots on a map! That's all homeplaces are to you. A heap you care what becomes of the poor folks who lives in them spots." Her voice was full of bitterness.

He looked grave when the dance brought them together again. "You're all wrong about this dam," he told her earnestly. "It's to help folks that it's being built, to keep—"

"Bird Hop Out and Crow Hop In!" came the call.

"It's being built to—" he began again.

"Gents Whirl!"

"How about sitting out the next set and talking this thing over?" he asked her as the couples began to break up.

"Can't!" She dashed across the hall, as if the set were promised, to where Paul and Linda and some high school boys and girls stood talking together.

She was afraid of this surveyor with his fine-sounding talk. Strangers who came around talking like that were always trying to put something crooked over on plain folks. That's what her father had always told her.

The next three sets were dances with classmates of Paul's, and Cynthia did not enjoy herself one bit. The boys talked about school affairs which meant nothing to her. They acted as if she were not only very young but very ignorant. It was a relief when Paul claimed her for another set.

"Hey! Not that way. We go left."

Oh dear! She was all mixed up, just because she had looked across the hall at the surveyor. Why did he watch her soberly like that, as if he had her on his mind? "Bet he thinks I'm a young lady seventeen or eighteen years old," she decided.

In a few minutes, he was at her elbow claiming the next set. "I want to tell you about this dam. You'll feel differently when you understand why it's being built." He was leading her to a seat.

She didn't want to "talk about that old dam nohow," didn't want to even think about it, she told him. She wanted to dance. Too polite to remind her that she was the one who had brought up the subject, he turned back with her to join the dancers. By the time Uncle Dan called "Promenade Away," she had learned a few things about this stranger. He came clear from Dicksville. He had graduated from State University there, and this was his first job.

"Will you be here next week?" he asked when he said goodnight to her.

She shook her head. "No telling when I'll get to another dance. I'm a stay-at-home girl."

"Well, I'll be seeing you again one of these days."

"More'n likely you won't."

"You're a funny little kid."

"How old do you think I am?"

"Let's see—my kid sister's twelve, and I'd say you were a little bit older, probably thirteen."

"I'm fourteen." She fled from him, humiliated. So, after putting up her hair and making up her face, she still looked like somebody's kid sister!

"Pa," said Paul suddenly, as they rolled along the black road toward home, "I want to go to the university and study engineering."

"Time enough to talk about that two years from now," said his father. "Time enough to change your mind, too."

"I want to build dams like this Lincoln Dam," he persisted. "You've no idea what a wonderful thing that is."

Cynthia sat quietly, conscious only of a bitter, numbing hate for a handsome young man with hazel eyes. He had been talking to Paul, making Paul discontented with his life on Brightwater Creek.

The girls decided to sleep on the upstairs porch and for a reason. There—if they shut the door—they could talk as long as they pleased, without anyone calling out, "Keep quiet, girls, and go to sleep." Neither of them wanted to sleep for hours.

"Don't see why we goes to bed noways," said Cynthia, "when we're as lively as that old hoot owl yonder." The tunes the Spruceville Music Makers had played kept repeating themselves over and over in her ears—teedle-dee, teedle-dum, teedle-deedle-deedle-dee. Now it was "Arkansas Traveler," and now "Sourwood Mountain," again "Cindy." She could hear Paul and the surveyor singing as they danced:

> "Git along home, Cindy, Cindy,
> Git along home, Cindy, Cindy,
> I'll marry you sometime."

Uncle Dan's fiddle still scraped away, and his sing-songing calls rang out: "Ladies Bow!" "Bird Hop Out and Crow Hop In!" "Promenade Away!"

"I liked Jim Holliday the best of anybody there, didn't you?" asked Linda.

"I hated him. He's got no business trafficking round here, putting on airs and talking like he read out of a book. Why can't he act natural?"

"He does, Cynthia. And he wasn't putting on airs. We sound as funny to him as he does to us. Some of the time, he couldn't make out what the folks were talking about, no more than if they talked French or Chinese."

Her bedfellow said nothing, and Linda chattered on. "Maybe I'll go to the university, too, someday. Maybe I'll be a teacher or a nurse or something."

"Oh, Linda!" The voice was almost a wail. "What do you and Paul want to leave your nice homeplace and go off down to Dicksville for?"

"But, Cynthia, we probably won't be living here more'n a year longer. I asked Jim Holliday about it tonight, told him near as I could where our house was. He said they hadn't finished surveying up this way yet, but he was almost sure that Brightwater Valley would be all under water when the dam was done."

"We'd all oughter refuse to move."

"What good would that do? We can't stop the water from rising. Anyway, I don't guess I'll mind as much as I thought I would." She was as calm as Cynthia was excited. "It'll be hard on Pa and Ma, but Paul and I want a different kind of life from theirs anyhow."

"You do? Well, I don't!"

"You wouldn't want to stay all your days up in Bee Tree Holler, would you?"

"I sure would—or else on Brightwater somewheres."

"Well, you'd get awful lonesome, even if you could. Your Pa and Ma won't live forever. Paul and I will be going away to school, and then we'll be getting married. Most all the other young folks will be going too, dam or no dam. Leastways, the ones who want to do anything."

"You and Paul have been a-listening to Jim Holliday. That's why you think you wants to git away from here. He's a slick talker. Tried to talk my ear off, too, but I wouldn't let him."

"I'm sleepy."

Cynthia turned her face to the wall. She was not sleepy, but a lump in her throat was nearly choking her, and she couldn't say another word without disgracing herself. Here was the hardest, sharpest-cornered fact she had ever faced—Linda and Paul and the other boys and girls who lived along Brightwater Creek and up in the hollows hereabouts would soon be grown-up and scattered like last year's birds.

Chapter 7

The Pryingest Man

"Shortcake for supper! Shortcake for supper!" sang Cynthia to herself. She was high in the mountainside pasture picking red raspberries. One last handful. There! Slowly she started down the hill, holding the heaped-up tin bucket carefully with both hands so that not a berry should roll off.

Just above the hickory tree, she stopped among the rhododendrons to look down into the yard. At the gate stood a mud-spattered black car. That meant one thing—a stranger. Nobody who knew the Bee Tree Hollow Road, with its hub-deep mudholes and ruts, ever tried to drive a car over it except in the driest weather.

A red trail of spilled berries lengthened behind Cynthia as she ran the rest of the way. The first person she saw was Granny, who sat idle on the bench outside the springhouse. Her ever-active hands were folded in her lap. Her eyes, usually bright and quick-glancing as a bird's, stared dully at nothing.

"Howdy, Granny. Ain't it pretty hot to be sitting in the sun?"

The woman on the bench did not hear her. She did not even notice that her grandchild was there.

Ma was in the kitchen, supposedly churning, but she

moved the dasher only now and then. She was listening to two voices—one Pa Bailey's, the other, a strange voice. "He's the pryingest man, Cynthy," she whispered, nodding her head toward the porch. "Asked your pa more questions than a census taker. And he's done gone all over the house from cellar to loft. Been in the barn and the woodshed and even poked his nose into the corncrib and the springhouse. You never heard nobody ask so many fool questions in your life. Listen to him."

Cynthia listened to a conversation that went like this:

"When was your house last shingled, Mr. Bailey?"

"What you want to know for?"

"As I told you, Mr. Bailey, I'm asking these questions in your own interest, to make sure that you are paid a fair price for your farm, that you get back the money and the work you've put into it." The man seemed to be trying hard not to lose his patience.

("Calls hisself an appraiser. What you reckon that is?" whispered Ma Bailey. Cynthia shook her head.)

"It's no business of the government's when I shingle my house, but I'll tell you. My pappy made them shingles twenty years ago, and I helped him put 'em on when the moon was waning. That's why they didn't never curl up much at the edges. They're as good today as they ever was."

"Have you made any repairs recently in any of your buildings?"

"How's that?"

"Have you painted or mended the house or barn or built new fences—anything like that?"

"No."

"What about the wallpaper in that front room? It looks new."

("He don't miss anything," whispered Ma.)

"Oh, the women done that."

("Now what you reckon he's writing in that little book of his?" Ma's whisper carried easily to the porch.)

The questions went on.

The answers got shorter and shorter.

Cynthia picked over her berries in silence, not missing a sound from the porch.

Now the chairs were scraping. The two on the porch were standing up.

Was the unwelcome visitor leaving?

Not yet. Enoch Bailey had some things to say to him.

"You tell the big boss down in the valley," he began, "that this homeplace ain't for sale and never will be noways. You tell him that Enoch Bailey is going to stay right here at the head of this holler, and his grandchildren and great-grandchildren are going to live right here when he's dead and gone."

"I understand the way you feel, and I sure wish that your great-grandchildren might make their home in this peaceful place. But what would they live on?"

"Live on? Why, on fatback and corn like anybody else."

"Mr. Bailey, there won't be enough soil left in these hollows and on these hillsides to keep anybody alive a hundred years from now, not at the rate it's being washed away. Anyway, there isn't a thing that you or I or anyone else can do to keep your farm from being flooded when the dam is finished."

"Some folks believes them stories, but I don't. I knows something about dams myself. You fellers are land-grabbing, that's all."

"Good day, Mr. Bailey." The stranger went out through the gate to his car. In a moment, he had started down the hollow.

"They'll never git me off my homeplace—never!" Enoch Bailey shouted after the machine.

The veins in his forehead stood out like a cord when he sat down to supper. His voice was still loud. "He's crazy, that feller is, crazy as old Aunt Dessie."

Cynthia looked into her father's deep-set eyes and saw fear—fear such as she had never before seen in his face.

Outside by the springhouse, Granny still sat looking into space. Ma had to call out, "Supper's ready, Granny," three times, and at last as loudly as she could, in order to make the old lady hear.

Chapter 8

The Baileys Go to Town

Next morning, as the clock in the steeple of the Spruceville Methodist Church pointed to eight-thirty, a farm wagon drawn by two bony mules drove up to the county courthouse. "Whoa-a!" Pa Bailey shouted in a voice high-pitched from excitement. He had put the coat of his one suit over his work shirt and overalls and topped his costume, as usual, with a wide-brimmed black felt hat. Jumping down from the high front seat, he tied the nigh mule to a hitching post. Granny and Ma climbed down laboriously. The old lady wore her best, though somewhat tarnished, black dress with a snow-white sunbonnet. Like her pioneer mother before her, she scorned hats. Mrs. Bailey's black straw hat rode high and unbecoming on top of her naturally slicked-back hair above a homemade dress of navy-blue rayon. Cynthia jumped out of the box of the wagon and shook the dust from the folds of her blue-and-white gingham. It was good to stretch. For more than two hours, she had been riding in a kitchen chair, with one hand clutching the side of the wagon and her feet braced to keep from pitching out over the wheel.

Enoch Bailey led off along the sidewalk and up the steps of the ugly brick building, followed by "his women." All walked with long strides and bent knees, as if crossing furrowed fields. Inside the musty hallway, they grew suddenly timid, peering about like deer who had ventured out of the forest into the open. Up the creaking stairs they went to a door inscribed

BENJAMIN JOHNSON Attorney-at-Law

Cautiously, Pa opened the door.

"Howdy folks, come right in." Mr. Johnson took his feet off the desk and removed his hat.

Mr. Bailey introduced himself and his family, then added, "My neighbor, Matt Wilson, he says you're the best lawyer 'round heres."

"You-all sit down," invited the lawyer, pulling four chairs into a semicircle in front of his desk. "Now, what's on your mind?"

"A whole heap's on my mind, Squire. Fifty year I've lived in Bee Tree Holler, peaceful and quiet-like. And now men have come tromping over my land, pulling my fences down, driving stakes into my pasture as if the place belonged to them. They nose around and ask questions that's nobody's business but mine. Folks tell me that 'most any day now, a stranger will come and offer me money and say, 'Take it and get out.'

"Some of the neighbors has took off to find them new homeplaces. But I knows, and you knows too, Squire, that no dam some thirty mile from Spruceville is going to back water clean to the head of Bee Tree Holler. What I wants you to tell me is this—do you know any reason why I can't sit right there and have the law on anybody that tries to put me off my own homeplace?"

The lawyer sighed. He had heard a story like this one so many times during the past few months. "You see, it's this way," he began patiently. "You can't have the law on men who are doing what the U.S. Congress has told them to do. That's how it is. These men who have come in here were given the right to buy a certain amount of land and build this dam. I know it's hard on you folks who have to move. I feel for you. Yet, someday, we'll all be glad this dam was built."

"Glad!"

"Yes, Mr. Bailey, I mean glad. Lincoln Dam will hold the water in the great river back, and make it work for us, and keep the small rivers and creeks from tearing down their banks and washing all our good soil down to the sea. In a few years, there'll be new factories in our towns, and boats will be steaming up and down the river, and folks that have just been keeping themselves and their children alive will prosper."

"What does us folks want with mills and ships?" Pa Bailey's voice was full of scorn. "A little bottomland, a cow, a pig, a coon dog, and a fishing line—that's all a body needs to be happy."

"It's the truth!" spoke up Granny like a wooden statue suddenly come to life.

"You'll get a fair price for your place," the lawyer went on, "enough to buy you a farm as good, and maybe better, than the one you've got now. You can tear down and carry off with you all the buildings, and you'll have time to raise this year's crop and maybe another.

"As for the water not coming into your hollow—don't fool yourself about that. My brother works on that dam, and he tells me those engineers have it all figured out to a foot—how high the water will rise in a flood, in a drought, and in between times. There's no guesswork about any of it."

Hope faded out of the four faces turned toward the man at the desk. Granny's eyes, usually like black jet beads, seemed to glaze over. For the first time in her life, she looked like a woman almost ninety years old. The little crosses around Ma's eyes deepened. Cynthia sat with her upper teeth clamped down on her lower lip, as if she were afraid to let go of it. Pa's lips were just a tight line. Quickly, he unfolded his long legs, stood, and drew out his ancient leather wallet. "How much do I owe you, Squire Johnson?"

"A friend of Matt Wilson's don't owe me a cent for a little talk like this. Sorry I can't do anything for you."

Enoch Bailey headed for the door, followed by his family. In silence, they went down the stairs. In silence, they climbed back into the wagon.

The return drive up over the hills always took longer than the outbound trip. Today, to the four people in the wagon, the distance had doubled. Also, the day seemed twice as hot now and the dust twice as suffocating. One-eye and Gideon refused to trot even on the level stretches of the hard-surfaced part of the road. Not till the mules had rounded the turn onto their own Hollow Road did they show signs of being half-alive. Then Ella stopped them.

She came running out of the cabin with wonderful news to tell them, her face a radiant contrast to the glum faces which looked down at her. "There was a man here today from Lincoln. He said Joe could have a job down there whenever he wanted to come. And we can live in one of them new houses with 'lectric lights and—"

"Git-up!" yelled Pa to the mules, without waiting to hear what else Ella and Joe would have in their new home.

Next morning, Cynthia noticed that the gun was back in its place over the shelf in the kitchen. "Leastways," she thought, "Pa's not fooling hisself no more."

Chapter 9

"Where's That Money At?"

"Pay to the order of Enoch Bailey fifteen hundred dollars."

Cynthia stared at the slip of paper in her father's hand. Yes—fifteen hundred dollars. That's what the check said. She tried to imagine what such an amount would look like in cash-money—silver dollars, half dollars, and two-bit pieces. Would it pave a shining path all the way to the gate? What could you buy with it? A fine house? Acres and acres of bottomland? The most money she had ever seen was forty dollars. That was when Pa sold a cow to Matt Wilson.

The Bailey homeplace was sold at last. House, barn, springhouse, holly trees, pasture, high rock—none of these things belonged to them anymore. A car was disappearing down the road. The man driving the car carried the place with him—that is, all legal rights to it.

"I had to take it. I had to," her father was saying, as if he had sold his soul. "There ain't no use holding out. That feller was Buddy Simpson. He used to live over on North Branch 'fore he growed up and went to college. He said exactly what the squire told us last summer, and Buddy wouldn't lie to me."

It was another spring. For a year, Enoch Bailey had sworn he'd never give in. The government couldn't take his home away from him—no-siree. Just let them try. This May afternoon, a tall, light-haired young man had driven up the road, strolled through the gate and out to the barn, and drawled, "I'm Buddy Simpson, Jim Simpson's boy. Remember me?" He had sat right down in the barn doorway with Pa and talked about the trout he used to catch in North Branch. Not until the older man seemed to regard him as a friend and neighbor did Buddy even mention Lincoln Dam or his business in Bee Tree Hollow. Then, long and quietly, he reasoned with the troubled man. Finally, Enoch Bailey had gone to the kitchen, fished from the cupboard a tin box, and handed over a yellowed paper—the deed to the old place.

Anyway, it was a heap of money, he told Mrs. Bailey and Cynthia, still acting as if he felt guilty. And they could take everything with them, every last thing they could tear down and carry off, and they didn't have to move for a year.

"I don't see no money," said Ma, who distrusted checks anyway and suspected young Simpson of being out to cheat them.

Pa insisted that the check must be good.

"Now, Enoch, because you knew his pappy ain't no sign Bud's not crooked. He was away down in the level land for years. Remember that. And he's working for that bunch down to Lincoln, ain't he?"

Enoch Bailey nodded.

"You go call him straight back and say you wants cash-money."

"I can't. He's done gone." Pa Bailey pointed to the cloud of dust far down the road. "Anyway, all I needs to do to git cash-money is take this paper to the bank."

Ma sniffed. She'd believe that when she saw the money, and not till then. And he'd got to catch the mule and go to Spruceville right now and get it and bring it home. Well, if it was too late today, he'd have to go the first thing in the morning.

Cynthia protested that it was dangerous to carry so much money around. A pickpocket could lift it off Pa before he could get home with it. The best thing to do was to take the money to the bank and leave it there.

At once her father and mother joined forces in the argument. Forty years ago, when Enoch Bailey was a boy, the bank at Spruceville had failed—a catastrophe which he had never forgotten. He would either keep this paper or get the money and bring it home.

"What will you do with all that money?"

"Hide it."

Suppose the house burned down. Then, Cynthia told them, there would be nothing to show for all they had in the world. Her father said he'd a sight rather take a chance on his house than on that Spruceville Bank. "Banks are safer now than they was," she insisted. The girl might as well have saved her breath for all the effect her talk had on either her father or her mother.

Now Granny stuck her head inside the door to say sharply, "Enoch, the next time one of them men comes riding up here trying to buy our timber, you run him off with a gun. We don't want no traffic with them." She went back to weeding and watering her sweet peas. Her hands, which a month ago had been as steady as Cynthia's, were trembling.

Poor Granny! Ever since the trip to Squire Johnson's office, she had seemed to fail every day. The past and present were hopelessly mixed up in her head. Sometimes her talk was of the days when the sides of Brushy Mountain were dark with virgin forests and lumber companies were sending their agents to buy up timber at the lowest prices the mountain people would take. Again, she was telling her son not to sell out to the railroad. When she was especially tired and confused, the old lady thought the Yankees were coming.

Only when she puttered about her flower garden did

Granny find peace. This she did early and late, watering the flower beds even when they were still damp from a shower, pulling up the tiniest weeds, transplanting plants from one bed to another, and then sometimes back to the original place. The very act of putting things in the earth gave her a comforting feeling that she would always be here.

Enoch Bailey got off early the next morning. By six o'clock he was trotting old One-eye down the mist-filled hollow. By one o'clock he was back again, pulling off the mule's bridle and turning him loose in the pasture. The only sign of the newly acquired "wealth" was a slight bulge in the back pocket of his faded overalls. In the kitchen, he pulled the money out with a flourish. What a small wad! Cynthia was frightened. Had he lost some of it already? Then her eyes widened. Fifteen one-hundred-dollar bills lay on the kitchen table. She hadn't known they made anything bigger than twenty dollar bills, and she'd seen very few of those in her life.

"Now, where are you going to hide it?" asked Ma Bailey in a half-whisper, as if afraid someone was listening.

Granny sat by the kitchen window in her favorite chair, rocking back and forth, smoking her pipe, talking to herself, and apparently paying no attention to the others. All at once she looked around excitedly, took her pipe out of her mouth, and shouted, "Hurry, Enoch! Git that money buried 'fore the Yankees come. And be sure you mark the place. Your Aunt Marthy never found them spoons she buried in the potato patch. And then the Yankees didn't come nowhere near her place on Sourwood Creek. But they're coming this time. I feels it in my bones." She looked far off into space again. Her voice dropped to almost a whisper as she conversed with herself.

Meanwhile, Mr. Bailey was taking down from the cupboard the tin box which had held the deed, a box so old that it was corroded and rusty. He put the bills into it and pressed the cover down tight. Then he opened the door of the warming closet by the chimney, reached far in, and tucked the box behind a loose board so that it lay between the cupboard and the bricks. This was the place where he had always hidden an extra bit of cash on rare occasions when he sold something for cash-money instead of trading it in at the store or the grist mill.

Cynthia looked on disapprovingly. "If the chimney takes fire the way it did two years ago, or the lightning comes down the chimney, the money would burn up even in that box, and then we wouldn't have a home, nor money to pay for a new one."

Pa rubbed his chin doubtfully. "Reckon we'll find a better place in the morning. We'll sleep on it."

To tell the truth, the Baileys didn't sleep much that night. They were all too conscious of those fifteen hundred-dollar bills tucked in by the chimney. Once Cynthia thought she heard someone prowling around the house. And every time she was awake, she heard her mother or her father coughing or a bed creaking.

Soon after midnight, thunder began to rumble faintly over back of Brushy. For two hours everything seemed to wait for the storm. Not even a leaf rustled. It broke with a mighty crash, which sounded right over the cabin, and the skies opened to let down a sheet of water. Everyone was awake now, and—with the possible exception of Granny—all were thinking of the same thing. Pa was just about on the point of going to the kitchen for the precious tin box and taking it to bed with him when the storm began to move its heavy artillery toward Sourwood Gap.

Everyone was glad when the night was over and the clouds above the mountain turned a soft pink, as if a thundercloud had never raised its ugly head up there. Pa was the first one in the kitchen. Fastening the straps of his overalls as he went, he headed straight for the chimney cupboard. He was going to put that money under a loose stone in the springhouse. The thunderstorm, he was sure, had been a warning that the present hiding place wasn't safe. Then, too, Ma had dreamed that a thief came and stole it. Maybe that was the Lord's warning, too.

Cynthia, in the midst of pulling her nightgown over her head, heard her father cry out as though in terrible pain. Thrusting her head back through the neck hole of the gown again, she ran into the kitchen.

There stood Pa with his arm thrust in back of the chimney cupboard, feeling, feeling with his fingers for a tin box, and saying over and over, "It's gone!"

"You lemme look," said Ma. "Men folks ain't never good at finding things." She reached her hand in and explored the niche between cupboard and bricks, even running her fingers into small crannies that could not possibly hold a box. She lighted a candle and peered in. Cynthia jumped up on a chair and went through the same motions as her father and mother had.

Granny came hurrying out of the front bedroom. "I'm afeered the rain done washed out that new rosebush Mattie give me," she said, as if that were the worst catastrophe that could happen to them all, and streaked out the door into the yard.

"Who could have been here? Who could have stole it?" Cynthia asked over and over. Then she dashed through the door and out to the gate to look for tracks. The storm had washed the ground clean of marks as completely as if a great roller had passed over it.

The puppies were chasing each other round and round in circles. The old lady was busily patting the wet earth around her rosebush, unconscious, like the puppies, of what went on around her.

It was just as well, thought Cynthia.

Chapter 10

Cynthia Makes a Resolve

To get to Uncle Mose's cabin from the head of Bee Tree Hollow, you take the trail up through the pasture, keeping on past High Rock, over the bald top of Brushy Mountain, and down the other side about twenty rabbit jumps, as Mose puts it. Two days after the disappearance of the fifteen hundred dollars, Cynthia followed the red-clay path to the hunchback's door. She did not look like the same girl who had so often before come up the mountain to talk things over with her uncle or to hear him tell stories. Dark rings made her eyes look twice their usual size. A deep line was cut between her eyebrows. Her pink dress was soiled and was missing two buttons. She had not glanced in a looking glass since this awful thing happened.

The hunchback looked more than ever like a gnome as he sat on the doorstep of his one-room cabin, knife in hand, transforming black walnut shells into buttons. Beside him sat a lifelike pair of owls he had carved from slabs of wood.

"Howdy, Cynthy," he called, then stopped with his knife in mid-air. "What in blazes has happened to you, child? You look like you'd walked out of a nightmare."

"I—I have, Uncle Mose." To her disgust, she burst into sobs.

"Cynthy, what is it? Ain't nobody dead at your house is there?"

"N-no, b-but we'd all be b-better off if'n we was dead."

"Now, now, you sit right down in this chair and rest yourself 'fore you tries to talk anymore." He led her to the cool shade of a great oak and pushed her gently into his own favorite seat, an armchair hollowed out of a stump. Giving her shoulder soothing pats, he hurried to the spring behind his cabin, carrying the weight of the girl's misery. Old Mose often said that he supposed there might be "a purtier, sweeter gal in the world than his niece Cynthy, but he didn't believe so." He'd a sight rather go through trouble himself than see her like this.

He came back with a gourd dripping with cold water. "Here, drink this." Now he began imitating the calls of the redbirds and the mockingbirds, luring them down from the trees and out of the brush to answer him, and to fly so close he could almost touch them. He called his pet squirrel and his tame crow and fed them from his hands. Cynthia looked on at this little act, as always, with delight. When she had stopped crying, the old man came and sat down cross-legged at her feet. "Now, you tell your Uncle Mose all about it. You ain't taking on this-a-way jest because your Pa's done sold your homeplace, are you?"

"It's worse'n that. Somebody's stole all the money we got—fifteen hundred dollars. Now we ain't got no home, no money, nor nothing. And what we're going to do, I don't know."

"Begin at the beginning and tell me the whole story clear."

She went back to the check and to Pa's trip to the bank and the hiding of the money.

"Who knew you had all that cash-money in the house?"

"Nobody exceptin' the man at the bank and—oh, yes—Sam and Mattie and Ella and Joe knew, of course."

"Who was in the bank when your pappy got the money?"

"I asked Pa about that. He said there was two or three

strangers in line ahead of him when he went up to that little winder—nobody he ever saw before."

"Has he told Sheriff Hall?"

"Yes. He rode right down to see him yesterday morning."

The old man was silent. Thinking.

"Cynthy, didn't you hear nobody moving around the cabin that night?"

"Seemed like I heard somebody once, but I thought it was Granny. She don't sleep much lately and prowls around a sight. Right after that, it thundered hard and drownded out everything."

"Didn't them fool pups bark?"

"No."

"They howl every time I comes around your place like I was a runaway jailbird. Don't they know enough to make a rumpus when a stranger comes trafficking around?"

"Oh, yes, they do, Uncle Mose. Lijer and Bijer are awful good watchdogs. But they was under the barn, most likely. They always hides in thunderstorms."

"Humph! Great watchdogs!" It was evident that the old man did not share Cynthia's enthusiasm for the hounds.

There was another silence.

"Does you recollect your Pa ever taking money out of that cubbyhole when anybody outside the family was there?"

She shook her head.

"You reckon Link Peters could have knowed where that money was at?"

"Link!" She started. "He ain't round here now, is he?"

"Yep! Out of jail and raring fer trouble."

The Peters family lived like a crowded nestful of eagles perched high in a small shack on the back side of Brushy, and they were as wild and as careless of the laws of men as eagles. Link, the oldest, was the head of the family—as much head as there was since old Rufe Peters died. If you added together all the days he had been to school in his nineteen years, they wouldn't total as much as the days he'd spent in jail. He'd been in twice for making moonshine and once for stealing from Calvin Fuller's store.

"Don't see how he could have knowed we had that money in the house."

"Somebody exceptin' your own folks must have knowed you had it and where you hid it."

Cynthia supposed so, doubtfully, but didn't see who it could be.

"Shore is a mystery, the way you tells it! Nobody knew you had the money. The thunder drownded out the noise the thief made and scared the pups so they didn't bark, and the rain washed out the thief's tracks."

The little man was silent. He turned over the walnut shell in his palm and studied it, as if the answer to the problem lay within the convolutions of the brown shell.

Then he said, "There's one ray of hope, as I looks at it. Nobody around these parts ever would have a hundred-dollar bill, lessen he'd stole some money or sold his farm. I never even seen one of them things in my life. The very first time the thief tries to bust one, he's a-goin' to get caught, shore. We'll watch and wait."

With this flicker of light to relieve the gloom, Cynthia had to be content as she started for home. As usual after a talk with Mose, she felt better. It wasn't so much what he said; it was that wise, prophetic air of his. In a moment, she turned back as if on a sudden impulse.

"Lend me two bits, will you, Uncle Mose?"

He couldn't for the life of him see what she would do with two bits on Brushy Mountain, but he cheerfully tossed her a quarter.

"Thanks. Goodbye."

This time she started in exactly the opposite direction, toward a wisp of blue smoke which floated up out of the woods a quarter mile below and behind Mose's cabin.

"Now, Cynthy," the hunchback called after her protestingly, "you'll git your head snapped off if'n you goes over there."

The girl went right on. The trail led into the deep woods, and she followed it until, presently, a clearing opened just big enough for a patch of corn and beans and two shacks. There was little difference between the shack inhabited by human beings and the one which housed the cow and the mule. Pigs wandered about the clearing unrestrained. So did young Peterses. At sight of the girl, the youngsters from the oldest to youngest took to the woods like a covey of partridges. Ma Peters, who was picking beans, stood her ground just as a mother partridge does.

Two mongrels flew at the visitor, half-barking, half-growling. The woman shouted curses at them until they slunk away.

"Howdy, Mrs. Peters."

"Howdy." It was more like a bark than a greeting.

"Hot, ain't it?"

"Yes."

"You got a bottle of that herb tonic you make handy?"

"Reckon so."

"I'd sure like some for Ma. She's been ailing ever since we lost all our money." Cynthia watched the brown, wrinkled face as she spoke. It might have been frozen for all the expression it showed.

"I'll fetch the tonic soon as I git my beans picked." With maddening deliberateness, and without speaking another word, Mrs. Peters filled up her basket then went into the shack. She did not invite the girl in—an amazing piece of rudeness for a mountain woman.

Emerging presently with a bottle of black-brown liquid, she held out her hand for the coin before surrendering it.

Cynthia, when she was back in the shelter of the woods, stopped and watched the clearing for a few moments. Within five minutes, the eight who had taken to the woods were back. Link was among them, and he and his mother seemed to be talking earnestly together.

"I wasted the two bits," Cynthia told Uncle Mose. She had already thrown the dirty liquid deep into a laurel patch. "I wanted to see how they'd look when they got a sight of me. But the young one—and Link, too—all took off. And that old woman don't show no more expression in her face than an Indian."

"I knowed you was wasting your time. Anyway, I'll keep an eye on Link."

The girl walked slowly down the mountain trail, as if she hated to get home. And she did. Home was not the pleasant place it had been in May when Pa strummed the banjo and made up songs, while Ma sang hymn tunes, and Granny seemed as young as any of them and twice as energetic. Even the puppies didn't play as much as they used to. Perhaps the hot weather made them dumpy, but Cynthia was sure they understood that the Baileys were in trouble.

A saddle horse was hitched to the gate. "Now who's here?" she wondered nervously.

Might be Sheriff Hall. No, his horse was darker than this one. The porch opened. A long-legged man wearing khaki slacks, a blue shirt, and a black felt hat appeared, followed by Pa. He was no stranger or foreigner—not in that hat. It was almost exactly like Pa's, even to its faded and battered look.

Mr. Bailey was following the visitor to the gate, and he was shouting so loud Cynthia could hear almost every word. "I tell you I ain't a-going to live on somebody else's land." The man untied his horse, swung into the saddle, and was off down the hollow.

Pa Bailey stood for a moment staring after him, then walked very slowly toward the barn. He stooped like an old man.

"Who was that?" Cynthia asked him.

"He's the feller who tries to tell farmers how they'd oughter raise their crops. Right now, he's offering to find me a place I can rent from somebody else. Kind of him, ain't it?" His voice was full of outraged pride.

"The county agent?"

"The same. I recollect when Amos Small was a young'un down here at the Brightwater School. Now he thinks he knows more'n I do because he went to college." Pa spat. "Cynthy, he actually thought I'd be a tenant or a sharecropper. Wanted to drive me down in his car to see a place way off yonder somewheres." He pointed to a gap in the hills.

"But what else can we do but rent a place, lessen we find our money?"

"I've got an idea, Cynthy. You know where that surveyor drove in the white stake?"

She nodded.

"The water ain't coming any higher than that. So I figure I'll tear down the house and barn and move them right up onto the mountain near Mose."

Cynthia threw back her head and laughed.

"I means it."

For a few moments she could not speak but only search his face. So he actually aimed to do such a thing! Live back in the woods like the Peterses! Scratch a little corn and a few beans out of the thin coating of soil on the rocks up there! How could he even think of such a life?

"We can't do that, Pa. We couldn't raise enough to feed ourselves. And how could we get to the store or the church house? How'd I go to school? It's twelve miles over the mountain to North Fork. We wouldn't see nobody but Uncle Mose and the Peterses."

"We could git to meeting sometimes, and we don't have to do right-smart trading at the store. And Cynthy, you don't aim to go to school after this year, does you?" He saw how her eyes clouded. "'Twouldn't be so bad as moving among strangers and living on somebody else's land, nohow," he added.

Nothing could be so dreadful as moving out into the unfamiliar world yonside the mountains without even a patch of ground to call your own. That was what Pa thought. Ma and Granny felt the same way. So had Cynthia until this very minute. Now she knew that a still more dreadful thing could happen to the Baileys. They could turn tail and crawl up Brushy Mountain and stay there like treed possums.

Chapter 11

A Hole in the Earth

So this was that "hole in the earth"! Cynthia hadn't been prepared for anything quite so big. She stood on Buzzard Mountain and looked down into a crater four hundred feet deep. The whole side of the mountain below her had been torn away. So had the side of Joe's Peak across the wide river. Terrifying sounds rose out of the depths. Thunder roared as dynamite exploded. Whistles screeched. Bells clanged. Truck horns honked.

Last year's tall tales were coming true fast. Linda, Paul, Cynthia, Bud Fuller, and Mr. Wilson had come down in the Wilson car to see for themselves the work on the great dam. The young folks were exclaiming and chattering excitedly—all except the girl from Bee Tree Hollow. She stared and listened and said not a word.

She had come into a land of giants—steel giants. The men down there were pygmies, swung about on derricks and cranes and pulled across the river in a cable car. One monster—Paul called it a steam shovel—gobbled up rocks and spit them out into trucks. High Rock—her throne back on Brushy—would just make a good mouthful for that thing. Another machine gnawed at the riverbed, bringing up loads of mud and stones in its dripping jaws. The girl shuddered.

Paul told her that the men could make those machines do exactly what they wanted done. The ones in the high tower were the big bosses. They telephoned their orders to men below, who carried them out with the help of all those machines. It still looked to her as if the steel giants were running things.

The boy was as full of information and enthusiasm as the driver of a sightseeing bus. "Just look at those concrete mixers. They turn out three cubic yards of concrete in a minute. That's what a guy told me. And you see those buckets of concrete? One of them—one, mind you—weighs twelve tons."

"You sound like a 'rithmetic lesson, Paul," said Cynthia disgustedly.

"We've got to come over some night and see this place all lit up," he went on. "The men work just like it was daytime, and I reckon it's brighter than day when they turn those big lights on. There's two thousand men working here, and—"

Cynthia was not listening now. She was trying to grasp for herself what was happening in these once-quiet hills. Here was a great river stopped short in its course, a river which used to go on rampages and spread destruction for miles. Now its power was nothing. Here were machines that made people look weak and silly. How ignorant the folks back home were! How little they knew what men could do when they got all their "contraptions" together!

She pictured her father pointing a gun at one of those men in the towers. A few words spoken into a telephone. A long iron arm would swing 'round, pick Pa up, and toss him to kingdom come like he was a stick. Then she imagined that stream of water turned on the little old cabin in Bee Tree Hollow. It crumbled into an insignificant heap of sticks and bricks.

Paul saw the terror in her face. "Why, Cynthia," he said. "What are you scared about? We're safe, way up here."

"I knows that. I knows too that men could wash away Brushy Mountain, if they set out to."

"Course they could. Didn't you know that till today?"

"No, and you didn't neither."

Paul irritated her. He had never used that I'm-older-than-you-and-I've-been-to-town manner on her before.

"I know more than you think I do about building dams. Someday, I'll be chief engineer on a job like this."

"What you want to do that for?"

"Why shouldn't he want to be an engineer?" Linda was definitely on the side of her brother.

Paul was silent. He was gazing out across the scarred earth with a far-off look in his eyes. He dreamed of the wonderful things he would do someday. To the Bee Tree Hollow girl, it seemed that a chasm as wide and deep as the hole below had opened between them today.

"When are we going to eat our victuals?" asked Mr. Wilson.

Linda opened the big box her mother had crammed full of food for them. At the sight of fried chicken, light bread, and cooking, all arguments ceased. The conversation turned to new subjects—who wanted dark meat and who wanted white, how many cookies there were, how many pickles, where was the salt. For a few minutes, the tremendous operations below became unimportant.

"And now," suggested Mr. Wilson, when the lunch box was empty, "why don't we see what Lincoln is like? They say it's bigger'n Spruceville."

Here was yet another wonder. A new town all complete, built for the people who worked on the dam, had risen as if at the wave of a wand where only fields and wooded hills had been a year ago. It had a main street and side streets, a schoolhouse, a church house, stores, and all the other things a respectable town should have.

"I thought it took years to build a town," said Cynthia. Her head bobbed from side to side as she tried to see everything.

"Nothing slow about this outfit," said Paul as proudly as if he had managed the undertaking himself.

They went into the new drugstore that didn't have a flyspeck on its marble counter and ate ice cream sodas with spoons as bright as the new spigots. Cynthia tried to make hers last as long as possible, taking tiny spoonfuls. A soda was a rare treat.

"Know what I want to do, Pa?" asked Paul suddenly. "I want to find the place where they hire men and ask them to give me a job for this summer. I could drive one of those trucks. And I bet I could learn to work a steam shovel or a jackhammer. But I'd like truck driving the best."

"I can give you plenty of work at home," said his father, but he was too easygoing to press the point, and Paul started off.

"I'm going to get me a job, too," decided Bud, and he followed after Paul.

Linda and Cynthia walked about the village. What a beautiful schoolhouse! They climbed the stone steps of the brick building and tried the front door. It was unlocked. Softly, they tiptoed in. What would it feel like, Cynthia wondered, to go to a shiny new schoolhouse like this? And what in the world were all these rooms for? Wide-eyed, she stared into the high-ceilinged, light-flooded classrooms, the amazing place Linda had said was a gymnasium, the tiled washrooms with fixtures as shining as the spigots at the drugstore soda fountain. Now, what was this room? It looked like a magazine-picture kitchen, but she didn't see why anybody would want to cook in school. Linda, who knew about domestic science classes and school lunches, explained.

"You mean they cook a hot dinner here for everybody?" Cynthia could hardly believe that.

Another room had benches along the walls and saws and planes and knives on the benches. Paul would love this room, they agreed.

The store windows along the main street fascinated both girls. How clean they were! And so full of fine-pretty things! Here was a church and over there a brick building marked COMMUNITY HOUSE, whatever that meant. And here was a new movie theater. Wouldn't they like to go to a show there! This building was labeled PUBLIC LIBRARY. They decided to go in and look around. Inside the door, Cynthia stood still and stared at the book-lined walls and up and down, row upon row, of bookcases.

The woman at the desk smiled at her. "Can I help you find something?" she asked.

"No'm. I ain't lost nothing. Never saw a whole place chock full of books before. I'd sure like to look at them."

"Just look around all you want to."

Now wasn't this something to see! She had heard of public libraries, but she'd no idea they were like this place. Why, there were literally thousands of books in this room. If she started right now and read the rest of her life, she couldn't get through a quarter of them. Some looked exciting, and some looked dull. Some were easy to read, and others she could not understand at all. There were books about places so far away, it didn't seem possible anybody from the United States had ever been there. At least a hundred were filled with stories—just stories. Then there were volumes with pictures in them, pictures so lovely she could hardly bear to close the covers and shut them away from her sight. If only she could take just one of them to put up on the wall of her room at home!

***

"Oh-h-h! Wouldn't you love to live in that house—the one with the red door? It's the prettiest house I ever saw."

"Give me that one yonder with the green door and the shiny knocker as yeller as gold."

The two girls were walking along a street of houses now, and they were as excited over the new houses as the boys had been over the engineering feats at the dam. Yet even the place with the green door couldn't compare to their own homeplaces, Cynthia insisted.

"Sometimes you sound as old as your Pa and Ma," said Linda.

When they came back to the car, the boys were waiting for them. Gone was the eager hopefulness from their faces. "The guy over there said I was too young to drive a truck or even work one of those cement puddlers. Offered me a job cutting brush back around Brightwater. I told him I was an experienced driver and a born mechanic, but he didn't seem to believe me." Paul's voice told of bitter disappointment. As for Bud, he was crushed.

"He wouldn't give me nothing to do."

They drove back over a wide concrete road, which a few months ago had been only two deep ruts in red clay.

"What in the world are those?" Cynthia pointed to a row of steel towers which marched, one behind the other, over the top of Bald Mountain and down the opposite side. A wide pathway had been slashed through deep woods to make way for the procession.

Mr. Wilson said it was a power line.

"Power line! What's that?"

Paul beat his father to the answer. "They're going to make electricity at the dam, and that cable will carry it for miles.

Those wires"—he pointed to the copper wires that gleamed red-gold in the sunlight between newly cut poles—"will take it to the farms and the villages."

He really did know a heap. She had to admit that.

"If we had that juice over our way," he went on, "Pa could push a button and get the cows milked; Ma could push another and have all the washing done for her—".

Cynthia broke out laughing as if he had told a funny story.

"What you laughing at, Silly? It's just the truth I'm telling. Don't you know there's an electric machine to do almost everything?"

The girl's head jerked suddenly around to look back. High against the sky loomed one of those steel towers, right beside a little old cabin. The cabin was like a child's toy house. Paul was looking back, too, but with hope, not fear, in his face.

On her way up from the Four Corners, the girl tried to put together into something which made sense all the bewildering impressions of the day. She couldn't do it. She couldn't give her father and mother much idea of what had happened, either.

"Must be the biggest hole anybody ever dug in the earth, sure enough," she told them.

"Them towers stood taller than the Methodist Church steeple in Spruceville." This was the tallest thing she could think of anywhere around here, but it didn't seem tall to her now and never would again.

"And the machines—" She stopped short. It was no use. She simply didn't have any words to describe their terrible power.

Suddenly her expression changed. "You oughter see that schoolhouse. It's like a palace. And the houses are so fine-pretty!"

"Reckon you'd like to live in Lincoln," said Pa disgustedly.

"Oh, no!" she protested. "I'd a sight rather live here always if I could. The houses are too close together. And the mountains are too far away."

A moment later she was saying, "Sure would be wonderful to go to a school like that. And borry books from that library! Never supposed there was so many books as that."

"Cynthy, you don't make sense. Sounds like you're plum mixed up."

Ma was right. The girl was all mixed up and all stirred up. She was going to feel that way for some time.

That night Cynthia dreamed that steel towers were chasing her over one mountain after another. She took refuge in a new house with a green door. The steel giants knocked the walls down on top of her.

Chapter 12

Dark Days

Those were dark days at the Bailey cabin, even if they were the longest and sunniest of June days. A month had gone by since the night when the fifteen hundred dollars had vanished, a month in which no clue whatsoever to the thief's identity had been discovered. Uncle Mose still "watched and waited" and suspected. So did Cynthia, but more and more hopelessly. The loss of the money seemed harder than ever to bear now that her father kept saying, "We'll have to move up on Brushy."

Granny was the only member of the family who did not worry. She seemed to have no idea what all the fuss was about. She would sit for hours at a time on the bench by the springhouse, looking as if her thoughts were far removed from the here and now. Still, her bright eyes were as keen and farsighted as ever.

"Cynthy," she called one morning, "who's all that coming up the holler?" She pointed to something far down the road which no one else had spied.

It was a truck, loaded with men and boys. As the truck came nearer, they saw that it bristled with axes and saws and clippers. The hounds sprang up and growled deep in their throats.

Pa Bailey dropped the armful of wood he was bringing into the house and reached the gate in a few long strides. Cynthia ran after him. Why, it was Paul Wilson. So that was it! Now she knew exactly what was going on. Paul had gone and taken that job cutting brush. This was one of the crews of men who were chopping down all the trees and bushes below the waterline on the government-owned land. And now the Bailey farm belonged to the government.

Why, oh why, did they have to begin work yet? As if the Baileys didn't feel homeless and upset enough without a gang taking possession of the whole hollow and turning it into a brush heap!

Mr. Bailey stood at his gate and eyed the cutting gang just the way the growling hound pups were eyeing them, and snapped out, "Howdy!"

The man at the wheel of the truck climbed down and explained what he and his men were going to do. He was sorry, he said, to have to begin the cutting while folks were still living here, but there were miles and miles of land to clear, and they wouldn't get it done in time if they waited for everybody to move out. Anyway, they wouldn't do anything to his fields and his yard till after he had gone away.

"It's your land! It ain't mine anymore." Pa shut his lips tight and turned quickly away as if he might say something he'd regret. Then he caught sight of Paul Wilson for the first time and swung around again.

"What do you think you're doing here?" All the anger and disappointment of the past month were in his voice and in the glance he fastened on poor Paul.

"You'd better shut your dogs up while we're working nearby," the man in charge interrupted. "They might get hurt."

Cynthia picked up the growling, struggling hounds, ran to the house with them, shut them in, and dashed back with the speed of a wind-blown flame. She had heard what her father was saying to Paul.

"You—you rattlesnake! Coming up here and making money out of a neighbor's sorry plight." Those were the first words she caught.

Paul's face turned crimson.

Cynthia waited, as one waits for lightning to strike. She wanted to cry out, "Don't say anything to him now, Paul." But she knew that it would only make both of them angrier.

"You can call me all the names you want to, Mr. Bailey, but I have to go where I am told to go, neighbors or no neighbors. Why don't you get a brush hook yourself and go to work here and get paid by the government, instead of taking on about your sorry plight?" It was Paul, so angry he didn't care what he said.

"You don't have no right to talk to my pa like that!" Now a third person was mad.

The boy did not answer her. He didn't need to. That swift glance flashed at her with his dark eyes said plainly what her father said a moment later: "You keep out of this."

"I'll do the talking," Pa told her. And he certainly did.

For three minutes straight he told Paul what he thought of him, of his pappy, and of his grandpappy before that. It was terrible to hear.

"Stop! Stop!" cried Cynthia. She couldn't stand any more. "You don't mean what you're saying. You knows you don't."

Enoch Bailey stopped, but only to get his breath and to tell Cynthia not to interfere with things that weren't her business. Then he said the worst thing of all. "I can't keep you from cutting brush on this land that's been took away from me, but I can keep you and all your family out of my house. And I will, and don't you or—"

"As if any of us would ever want to come here after this!" the boy interrupted. His face was dead white now. He slashed viciously at a clump of laurel with his brush hook.

"And Cynthy," went on Pa Bailey, "you ain't to go down to the Wilsons' no more."

Now the girl's face was white.

Paul went to work as far as possible from the house.

The gate banged behind Cynthia. She fled from Pa and Ma and Paul and the sight of Bee Tree Hollow being shorn of its green beauty. Up on High Rock alone between Brushy Mountain and the summer sky, she studied how to undo all the harm that had just been done. What should she do? Write to Paul? But she couldn't unsay the dreadful things that had been said. Anyway, the trouble was not only what had happened today. She and Paul and Linda somehow clashed nowadays. There wasn't that same togetherness they always used to feel. And it was all the fault of that dam. Lincoln Dam had taken away her home. Now it was taking the two best friends she had in the world. What was left?

She did not go down the hill at dinner time. She wasn't hungry. All the long summer afternoon she sat on the hemlock-shaded rock and thought until her head ached. She still didn't know how to put a broken friendship together again. Not till the hollow was all in shadow did she stop perching up there like a lone bird, swing herself down, and follow the trail back through the woods. At the pasture gate, she stopped and took a long look down the hollow. The dark green laurel and rhododendron and the light green azalea and dogwood bushes, which had banked both sides of the red clay road, lay flat on the ground as far as she could see.

Right after supper, the girl made an excuse for going to see Mattie. The person she really wanted to see was her oldest nephew. Cornering Dan at the gate, she held under his nose a dime from her own horde of slowly acquired silver. "I'll give you this if you will jump on Gideon and ride down to Wilsons' with a letter."

Dan lost no time starting out to catch Gideon. There were months between the dimes he saw and could call his own.

"Now be sure you offers to fetch back an answer," she told him when he started off bareback.

Mattie had stopped in the middle of washing the supper dishes to ask Cynthia questions. Had they heard anything from Sheriff Hall? What were the folks going to do about a new homeplace now? Was Pa really going to move up beside Uncle Mose?

"I don't know," said the girl to all questions, only half hearing what her sister-in-law was saying. Her troubled blue eyes scarcely left the road once from the moment the boy and mule went trotting out of sight. And in her thoughts, she was going over and over the brief note which was traveling in the pocket of the boy's overalls.

Dear Paul:
This is to tell you I am terribly sorry about this morning. Pa said things he never meant because he is so upset nowadays. I can't come down and see you and Linda now, but I hope when Pa cools off, we can be together some more and go on like this never did happen.
Your friend,
Cynthia

Dan was gone an hour, and each of that hour's quarters seemed like a whole hour. "I got an answer," he called out as proudly as if he had written it himself.

To Mattie's and Sam's and Dan's disappointment, Cynthia did not open the letter there. Instead, she tucked it into the front of her dress and hurried on up the hollow. Not until she was out of sight did she open it and read:

Dear Cynthia:
Just forget it. You and Linda and I probably won't be seeing each other after this summer anyway. Pa has bought a farm yonside Lincoln about ten miles. We'll move as soon as the crops are in, and Linda and I will go to that new school in Lincoln.
So long and good luck,
Paul

Cynthia tore the paper into little pieces and let the breeze strew them like flakes of snow over the road and the heaps of withering bushes beside the road.

Chapter 13

A New Teacher at Brightwater School

It was the first day of school. And it was the last year there would be a Brightwater School. Cynthia hurried down the red clay road. The short brown curls that usually ran wild about her face were held back neatly by combs with blue bows on them—a present from Ella. She wore a new blue "store-bought" dress, also contributed by Ella. "Little Cynthy" was growing tall. The dresses she had worn in the spring were all too short, even with the hems let down.

She was hurrying because she wanted to see the new teacher—this woman who was coming all the way from Dicksville to teach on Brightwater Creek. Was she young? Was she pretty? Would she understand—oh, would she—that some girls just naturally had a terrible time with arithmetic? Or would she be like Miss Peck, who had taught the Brightwater School for years and years? She thought Cynthia was stupid and lazy. She couldn't see that a girl might get so discouraged that it didn't seem any use to try anymore, especially a girl who lived at the head of Bee Tree Hollow and had to miss school a heap of the time in winter.

All at once her feet began to drag. There would be no Linda waiting in the schoolyard to talk to her! The Wilsons were moving in two weeks, so Bud Fuller had told her. Even if Linda were there, she wouldn't be talking to Cynthia Bailey—not anymore. The Wheelers would be gone, too. They had moved to Shady Valley.

Everything was changing fast. The little cabin at the corner was empty. No Ella watched the road from her porch, and no Joe eased the time away. They had moved to Lincoln last month. Already the place looked forlorn. A windowpane was broken out and another cracked. Tall weeds grew around the door, and a woodchuck took a sunbath on the doorstep. At the mill, no creaking wheel turned, and no mules stood stamping while wagonloads of corn were being ground. The gate of the Wheeler house flapped back and forth, banging disconsolately in the breeze.

In the schoolyard, about a dozen children were playing. They were all younger than Cynthia, at least all but one—a girl in a cherry-colored sweater who was batting a softball.

"Good morning," said the girl in the bright sweater as the girl from Bee Tree Hollow walked into the schoolyard. "I'm Mary Rogers, and I reckon you're Cynthia Bailey." Why, this was the new teacher, and she acted as if she were giving a party and Cynthia was a welcome guest. "You live the farthest away of all the boys and girls, don't you?"

"Yes'm. Up to the head of Bee Tree."

"It must be hard for you to get here some days, isn't it?"

"Yes'm. It sure is."

In a few moments, the bell was ringing. Then began the bustle of choosing seats, of helping to give out books and pencils and filling inkwells. After that came the fun of watching to see what the new teacher would do next and next.

As soon as the novelty of all this wore off, Cynthia began to realize that something hurt inside her. It was like the kind of toothache that does not hurt all the time but gives a jab at one's jaw every now and then. No Linda sat across the aisle to exchange glances with when something funny happened. Jab. There would be no Linda to eat lunch with. Jab. The worst twinge of all came when she thought of school letting out. Always the two girls had taken turns walking partway home with each other. One night Linda would go as far as the Four Corners with her, and the next Cynthia would walk down-creek with Linda as far as the big oak. Then they would talk over everything that had happened all day. "You two are the talkingest gals in ten counties," Ma Bailey often said. It was probably true. Certainly, Cynthia had never talked with anyone else so much, unless perhaps with Paul. Jab. Ouch. Oh well, she was just a backward little backwoods girl to them now, if they ever gave her a thought.

"Cynthia!"

School was out. The Bee Tree Hollow girl was leaving the schoolyard. She turned at the sound of her name. It was the new teacher calling to her. "May I talk with you a moment?"

What had she done? It couldn't be anything terrible, or Miss Rogers wouldn't sound so pleasant.

"You've had to stay out of school a great deal, haven't you?"

"Yes'm. Right-smart. But most of the time, I couldn't help it. After a big rain, that holler is mud a foot deep. I can't git here withouten I rides One-eye, and Pa uses him to haul wood."

"I know. And when you come back, it's easy for you to make up what you've missed, except arithmetic. Isn't that so?"

"Yes, Ma'am." Now, how did she know that?

"And you've begun to feel sort of hopeless about catching up?"

Cynthia nodded. This woman didn't need to ask you questions. She knew the answers already.

"Would you like to go to high school next term?"

"Oh, yes'm, I would." All of a sudden, Cynthia realized, to her own surprise, that she really did want to keep on going to school. "Only—" How could there ever be any more school for her if the Baileys moved up on Brushy Mountain?

"Only what?"

"Don't see how I can get there noways."

The teacher brushed the doubt aside quickly. "A girl like you will find a way to do the things she feels she must do. Now, what I want to know is whether you'd like to have me help you catch up in arithmetic so that you'll be ready for high school next year. I'm sure you can be if you're willing to stay one night a week after school."

Somehow, looking into the teacher's face, Cynthia believed that she could find a way to do almost anything. "I'll stay," she said.

Her step was as light as the touch of a leaf on the road going home, and her heart was lighter than it had been for many a day. In spite of all the changes, school was going to be fun this year. And in her ears sounded a bugle call into action: A girl like you will find a way to do the things she must do.

It seemed only a few minutes before she had covered the three miles between school and Sam's house. Here, everything was the same except that the baby was walking now. Probably this cabin would be empty by wintertime. Sam was hunting for a new home. Almost every week lately, he had been to look at a place with Amos Small. However, Cynthia suspected that her brother, like some other home-hunters, was not in any hurry. Jaunting around in the county agent's car was more fun than anything he had ever done before in his quiet life, and he wanted the fun to last a while.

The sound of staccato hoofbeats broke in on her thoughts. Someone was coming down the hollow at a gallop. Why, it was Pa! On One-eye! She didn't know the old mule could go like that. Mule and rider did not slow down when they met her.

"I'm a-going after Doc Collins," called her father as he dashed by. He was breathing as hard as if he were doing the galloping. "Your granny's had a stroke. You hurry home and help your ma."

Lijer and Bijer came leaping over the fence and tore down the road to meet her, as usual, wagging ecstatic greetings. What was the matter with their mistress? She did not run or throw sticks for them to retrieve, or even pat their brown and white satin heads.

Chapter 14

Granny Tries to Talk

"I'm mighty glad your grandma is better, Cynthia," said the teacher. "Would you like to stay tonight and tackle arithmetic?"

"Yes'm, I reckon so." How she dreaded "tackling" this arithmetic drill! It meant showing the new teacher how little she knew!

School had been in session a week. And what a week it had been for Cynthia! Through one tense night, nobody in the Bailey cabin had slept. For two days and nights, someone had had to sit by Granny's bed every minute. During that time, Cynthia had stayed out of school, and the rest of the week, she had hurried home the minute school let out to wash the stacked-up breakfast and dinner dishes and to cook supper. The pink was gone from her cheeks. There was a droop in her tired shoulders.

"And now let's review decimals," suggested Miss Rogers brightly, as if decimals were some game. She proceeded to work miracle after miracle. First, she turned a half hour into a quarter of an hour. At least it seemed like no more than fifteen minutes. Then she actually did turn decimal fractions into a game, played merrily on the blackboard. Greatest miracle of all—Cynthia didn't feel stupid anymore, not even when she made bad mistakes. As Miss Rogers said, she was quick at everything but arithmetic. That was the only subject which held her back with the younger boys and girls. "You just got stuck, that's all, and you'll soon catch up," the new teacher told her understandingly.

"There's one more thing you need to brush up in a little," she said when the arithmetic lesson was over. "That's grammar. You see—" She spoke gently, as if afraid she might hurt the girl's feelings. "You write much better than you talk."

"I knows it," said Cynthia. She blushed. The girl knew that when she had a pencil in her hand, words formed in the patterns she had learned at school, but when she opened her mouth, words came out much the way her father and mother talked at home.

"I want you to put these four cards up somewhere in your room. Practice saying the top line on each one over and over. Next week, I'll give you four more if you'd like me to."

Cynthia took the cards. On each were two lines, the first written in red ink and the second in black, one labeled *right*, the other *wrong*. The top card read:

Right—I don't aim to do any work Saturday.
Wrong—I don't aim to do no work Saturday noways.

On the walk home, the girl began repeating the red lines over and over to herself. Ambition surged like a tide within her. She wasn't stupid. She wasn't. She was going to school somehow, even after the Brightwater School was gone. The more she heard her father talk of backing up onto Brushy Mountain, the more determined Cynthia was not to "take to the woods." Though she did not know it, the Baileys' "least child" was growing up fast.

Footsteps sounded on the road. She turned to see Mose hurrying to overtake her. Even with a pokeful of groceries slung over his back, he could cover the ground faster than she could without running.

"Howdy, Cynthy. Hear your grandmammy's getting better. She'll live to be a hundred yet."

"I reckon so. The doctor says, might be she'd even walk again with a cane. You know, Uncle Mose, I think her head's clearer now than afore she was sick. If she could only talk! It's awful to listen to her trying and trying to tell us things and just making sounds like a baby."

Mose clucked sympathetically, then asked, "What you suppose I heard at the store?"

His news was that Link Peters had gone to Dicksville. Leastways, that was where he had told Cal Fuller he was going. Of course, he might have been lying. Now, where did he get the money even to pay his fare? That's what Mose wanted to know. "Wait till he tries to break one of them hundred dollar bills, and see how quick the sheriff gets him!" he prophesied.

At these words, a hope that had almost died stirred inside her. "Oh, Uncle Mose! If we could only get that money back!"

"Watch and wait," counseled the old man, and he went dogtrotting on ahead of her. It seemed to the girl that she had watched and waited for a long time.

Ma Bailey stood at the kitchen door peering down the road. She looked relieved at the sight of Cynthia.

"I wish you'd go in and see your granny. All day she's been a-trying to tell me something. All it sounds like to me is 'Pick' something or other. Whether it's apples or tomaters or flowers she wants me to pick, I can't study out. See if'n you can tell what's worrying her so."

The girl went at once into the front bedroom. The old lady lay very still under a bright patchwork bed-quilt. Her face had grown thin and transparent but was still brown with tan, so that she looked like one of the dry brown leaves which were already beginning to fall in the yard.

"Howdy, Granny."

The old lady made noises that sounded like, "Howdy, Cyn."

"Ma says there's something you wants us to pick. Is it the tomaters?"

"N-no! N-no! D-d-d—" She made such an effort to say the word that drops of sweat stood out on her forehead along the edges of her white hair.

And Cynthia tried so hard to understand that her head ached.

Finally, Granny raised one arm with a tremendous effort and crooked a thin finger toward the window, pointing outside and down toward the ground.

The girl looked out. Under the sill, Granny's new rosebush raised its one slender stalk hopefully. It was the bush the old lady had fussed over so much last summer. Poor soul! She must have the idea that it was in blossom.

"Sorry, Granny, there's nothing to pick now. The little bush won't blossom again till next spring."

The lips in the brown face on the pillow kept moving, but no intelligible sounds came out. The eyes said plainly, "Why can't you understand? I'm trying to tell you something terribly important." Then, in a few moments, the eyelids closed. Worn out with the effort to make herself understood, she slept.

The next day Granny wasn't so well, and she seemed to have forgotten whatever it was she had tried to say.

Chapter 15

Left Alone in the Hollow

A cloud of red dust rose behind a mule team and wagon as it turned onto the Brightwater Road at the Four Corners. Cynthia and Pa and Ma Bailey stood in the middle of Bee Tree Road and waved as long as any sign of a wagon was visible. Then they turned and started home without speaking.

Sam and Mattie and the children had moved away.

The hollow seemed all at once a place of desolation. On Brushy Mountain the maples had unfurled scarlet banners. But the three people could not see the beauty high up there. They were looking at a chimney rising stark and lonesome in a littered yard—all that was left of Sam's place.

Cynthia tried to be cheerful. "Sam'll be coming back tomorrer or next day to bring One-eye home. And then he'll be back again to help pick apples and peaches. I reckon they'll be visiting us often. Mattie said they aimed to."

Mrs. Bailey blew her nose.

Mr. Bailey said nothing.

Cynthia gave up.

"'Taint right for families to be scattered, nohow," Ma burst out suddenly.

Now Pa reached the explosion point, too. "Sam living in

Spruceville! Working in a garage! What kind of life is that for a boy who's always had a piece of land of his own?"

Cynthia said nothing more out loud. She was carrying on a conversation with herself.

"Are we Baileys a-going to stay on here till everybody else is gone?"

"Not if I can help it!"

"Are we a-going to move up on Brushy?"

"Never!"

On the very next Saturday, the Bee Tree Hollow girl saw another family vanish behind a curtain of dust. This time she watched from a distance. This time she did not wave her hand. And today she could not have thought of anything cheerful to say if her life depended on it.

Hidden by the trunk of a great tree on the bank of Brightwater, she had watched the Wilsons dashing from house to car with bags, boxes, and suitcases and the kitchen clock and finally all climbing into the car with the cat and the dog and driving off behind the last load of goods. Not till she was sure they were gone and wouldn't come back did she leave her hiding place and continue down the road to the big house with the belfry on the roof. Then she stood in the yard and stared.

Could this be the old Wilson homeplace—this empty house with blank windows and rubbish-strewn yard? It was a dead home—dead as the ashes that lay on the wide hearth inside. She fled to the garden. Here at least the old trees were still standing, even though most of the plants and shrubs had been dug up and carried away. And here was that old wooden bench! Dead leaves and pine needles lay thick upon it. She brushed them away. Deep and inerasable in the silvery wood were the initials of those boys and girls who had surprised Paul on his sixteenth birthday. Here, in one corner, were C.B., L.W., and P.W., as if the three of them belonged together. In this neat column, the Wheelers had cut their initials. B.F.—that

Cynthia of Bee Tree Hollow

was for Bud Fuller. L.E.D. and W.M.D.—now who were they? Oh yes, she remembered, the cousins from Shady Valley.

And Paul had said that he would keep this seat always and take it with him if they moved away!

The girl could not see the letters anymore. Her eyes were blinded. Leaning as if for comfort against the wrinkled gray bark of the tree, she did what she had been wanting to do for weeks—let herself break down and cry. It was a good chance. She was all alone with a deserted house in a deserted garden. At least she thought so.

"You'll be seeing them again," said a voice.

Looking up with a start, she saw through her tears a tall, tanned man in khaki, who looked somehow familiar. Why, it was that surveyor Jim Holliday!

"I don't want to see you. You've spoiled my whole life—you and your old dam!" The girl jumped up as if she would flee from the sight of him.

He blocked her way. "Now look here, Cynthia Bailey, don't be a little fool. A dam can't spoil your life, and I can't either. And—" He broke off abruptly as he looked into her eyes. Blue eyes like those shouldn't be clouded and have hollows under them any more than a June sky should be gray.

"What makes you look like that?"

"Like what?"

"Like a girl turned into a little old woman. What's been happening to you?"

"Plenty!"

"Want to tell your Uncle Jim all about it?"

To her surprise, she found she did.

For fifteen minutes Cynthia didn't stop talking, except to catch her breath and take a fresh start. She got everything in—the sale of the house, the disappearance of the money, Granny's sickness, Pa's determination to be a squatter on Brushy Mountain, the quarrel with Paul, the new teacher, arithmetic lessons, the new ambitions which stirred within her—how she wanted to go to high school and maybe even to college and to read lots of books and have a new homeplace.

Until now the girl hadn't realized herself quite how much her hopes for the future had changed during these past months.

At last her story was told. Out shot Jim Holliday's hand. "Shake!" he said. "Stood right up to all these things that have happened, didn't you? And you've grown up, Cynthia. I'll never call you a little girl again."

Sweeter words never fell on the ears of a girl who was small and backward for her years.

And now he wanted to do the talking. He told her that this dam or another like it had to come sooner or later if folks were to go on living among these hills. Someone had to harness this river and make it work for man instead of against him. Someone had to find ways to make the thin, worn-out soil richer, just as those men down at Lincoln were doing. And someone had to plant trees on cut-over, eroded hills, which was exactly what gangs of men were beginning to do.

"And you're going to have a new homeplace. If you folks don't get on the track of that thief, you can borrow some money, buy a piece of land, and move your old buildings. I know any number of people who will put up a loan when they've heard the story you just told me."

Her smile was lovely to see. "Didn't have any idea you were such a kind man. And Pa called you a skunk!"

"I'm not being kind. I'm just thinking of the whopping big job you've got ahead of you. I want to see you get ready for it."

"A big job? Ahead of me?" Her eyes opened wide in amazement.

"Yes, Cynthia. All the king's horses and all the king's men can't do it, but maybe people like you can."

She laughed. Jim Holliday was just talking nonsense after all. Yet he didn't even smile.

"Haven't you even heard about the dictator chaps?"

"Oh—them! Hitler and Mussolini?"

"Yes, and there are plenty of others trying to do the same things they did, or just waiting their chance. They keep popping up—even here in America. Men who make people hate each other and fight each other. I tell you, Cynthia, folks like you are desperately needed in this upset, muddled-up old world."

Now she saw how deadly in earnest he was. All the usual joking, teasing tone was gone out of his voice. But what did he mean? "Why folks like me?" she asked in a puzzled tone.

He looked into her clear, searching eyes. "Because it's going to be hard for the big talkers to fool you, and still harder for them to make you hate other people. Because you don't care too much about tinsel pretties and having things easy, and never will."

"But what can I do about the world?"

"Nothing right now, except what you are doing." He unfolded his long legs and stood up. "I reckon this is the end of old Parson Jim's sermon for today." He started down the brick-paved path, then stopped and turned around. "You aren't going to lose as much as you think when you move. You'll take the best things right along with you."

She sat silent for a moment, thinking over what he had said. "You mean I've got them inside me?"

"That's it! And don't worry too much about losing Linda and Paul either. They'll get homesick for you and Brightwater. Wait and see if they don't. So long."

He swung off down the creek.

The girl sat for a full minute and stared after him, saying over and over to herself, "I've grown up! Folks like me are needed." Then she started for home at a brisk walk, turning to gaze out over Turkey Hill, over the blue mountains beyond, but not once looking back at the empty house and deserted garden.

Chapter 16

"I Have to Find a Homeplace"

Amos Small came quickly out of his house on lower Brightwater, jumped into his car, and started out of the yard. Suddenly, he swerved and landed in the ditch. "You fool, you! Are you trying to get yourself or me killed?" he shouted at the white-faced girl in blue who stood in the middle of the road.

"I had to stop you," she said. "I've walked all the way from the head of Bee Tree Hollow to see you."

"Don't you ever in all your life run out in front of a car like that!"

The girl did not seem to hear what he was saying.

"Mr. Small, I have to find a new homeplace. I can't live yonside of nowhere and never go to school and never—"

The county agent gave up trying to talk to this girl and went to the barn for a shovel. His car had to be dug out of the ditch. That was certain.

"You see," Cynthia went on as soon as he was back with the shovel, "if we move up over Brushy, like Pa aims to, we'll always be backwoods folks, and I'll never get to high school."

"Who are you?"

"Cynthia Bailey."

Mr. Small sighed. So this was Enoch Bailey's daughter. Hadn't he talked himself hoarse to Bailey more than once? The man was as stubborn as that old one-eyed mule of his. How on earth could he be expected to do anything for a man who had lost all his money and yet refused to face that fact and work somebody else's land?

"I'm sorry, but I don't see how I—" He looked up and saw her face and knew he couldn't drive off and leave her.

"Hop in!" he said, when the car was back on the road again. "I have to be in Spruceville by nine, but we can talk on the way."

Cynthia did all the talking. Mr. Small had no chance for a word. She knew now, she told him, just what must be done. It had all come to her suddenly last night in bed. She would find a piece of rich bottomland somewhere and borrow the money to buy it for her father. Pa loved good land. That was the one thing which would make him give up this idea of joining Uncle Mose on Brushy—a chance to own a nice little farm of his own where he could raise a real crop. Of course, it couldn't be just anywhere, like that place. She pointed to the neat farmhouse they were passing on the Spruceville Road. Her folks had to be off by themselves a little bit, with hills for company. They would be terribly lonesome on level land and with other folks living close to them. Yet the new place would have to be where she could get to school, even in winter. She couldn't lose any more time on account of bad weather and mud.

They didn't need to buy a house. Her father could move the old one and all the other buildings to this new place, just as he was planning to haul them up the mountain. Didn't Mr. Small think it was a fine idea?

The county agent's forehead was deep-creased by now. Ye-es, it was a fine idea. How was he going to say to this girl what he had to—that she was daydreaming, that there was scarcely any good bottomland for sale now in this whole country, except in some backwater far from any school, so long had the Baileys waited.

"If you'd come to me a few months ago, I might—" he began.

"I'll work vacations to help Pa pay back the money, and in a few years, we'll own it clear." Her face was shining as she went on planning without hearing a word Mr. Small said.

"Wait a minute!" he commanded. "I can't just conjure up a farm. Right now I don't recollect a piece of land for sale that comes anywhere near your specifications."

"Not even a little piece?"

Mr. Small wished the Bailey girl would stop looking at him like that. Oh well, after he'd done his business in Spruceville, he'd drive her around a little and let her see for herself.

Arrived at the county seat, Cynthia started walking down the main street while the county agent attended to his affairs. She did not get far. Here, in a store window, a machine was doing a washing all by itself. One could see the clothes sloshing about and soapsuds foaming all over them. Presently, a woman came and pressed a button. The sloshing stopped. She pressed something else, and the water ran out. Then out came clean clothes. Was it a trick? Could washing be that easy? No lugging pails of water from the springhouse. No rubbing and scrubbing on a washboard. Why, this must be one of the electric washing machines Paul had talked about.

How Ma needed a machine like that, now that Granny wasn't able to help her anymore! Someday, she would have to work to pay for a contraption like that.

A half hour later, Mr. Small found his passenger still staring into the window and still wondering how long she would have to work to pay for a contraption like that.

"Now," he said, not too hopefully, "we'll drive around and see what we can find."

He drove up West Fork and to Blackwater Brook, then to North Fork, and after that over Red Mountain to Shady Valley. Cynthia's hopes were like waves breaking on the seashore.

They kept rolling up, only to go ker-plop. A piece of bottomland at West Fork which looked promising had just been sold. A little parcel of land with an old cabin on it yonside Red Mountain was for sale, but there was no water to be had. Still another was owned by a man nobody wanted for a neighbor.

"That's a real homeplace," said the girl as they drove by a cabin perched on a lower slope of Strawberry Hill above a strip of bottomland. "Pa and Ma would sure like that. Could I get to school from here?"

The answer was no.

The county agent drove on back to the Spruceville Road and headed the car toward Brightwater. Then, as if suddenly remembering something, he turned up a little-traveled dirt road.

"Oh!" exclaimed Cynthia at the sight of a neat cabin set on a wedge of bottomland.

"Don't get excited," Mr. Small told her. "You can't buy Lem Matthews' place, but there's a bare chance that I can talk him into selling you a little piece of land. He's got more than he can take care of."

A white-haired old man sat on the porch whittling an ax handle out of an ash stick. "Howdy, Lem. I was over this way, and I thought I'd stop and see how your rheumatism was." Mr. Small strolled casually up on the porch as if business of any kind was the last thing in the world on his mind.

Lem's woman appeared briefly at the door to greet the visitor and ask if he and "the gal" wouldn't stop and have some dinner. The county agent said he had to be going right along, then sat down and talked with the old man for half an hour about the weather, the state of roads, local crime—everything except selling land.

When he rose to leave, Mr. Small stood for a moment looking down across the bottomland, which stretched from the cabin almost to the Spruceville Road. "Don't see, Lem, how you take care of all this land with your rheumatism so bad."

"I don't half take keer of it. Land's all growing up to brush and briars."

The visitor asked if he'd ever thought of selling a parcel.

The old man said he'd hate to have a neighbor so close.

"I can find some nice folks to buy it if you want to sell—one of those families that are going to be flooded out next summer."

"We-e-ell—"

"Think it over. So long, Lem."

Cynthia was disappointed that the county agent left at that point. "No use urging the old fellow," he explained. "He's got to have time to get used to the idea of sharing that little farm with somebody else. I'll drop around in a week and see how he feels then."

He drove her home as far as Brightwater Four Corners. "I'll let you know as soon as Lem makes up his mind one way or the other. But don't you go and get your hopes up. He's a lot like your Pa when it comes to doing something different from what he's always done."

"I'll keep my hopes down," said the girl with a laugh. "Thank you for your trouble."

He put his foot on the starter, then took it off again. "Cynthia," he called.

She turned back to the car.

"Cynthia, you don't have to bury yourself up on any mountainside, even if your folks do. I'm certain I could find a place in Spruceville where you could work for your keep and go to high school."

She was silent. A terrific struggle was going on inside her. Finally, she said with firmness, "I can't do that—leastways, not yet." The look in her face was almost desperate. "I'm obliged to see them through this—this—" She groped for words to express what leaving Bee Tree Hollow meant to her father and mother. "It's like the end of the world for them. That's what it is!"

What wouldn't he give, he thought, to find for her that "nice little farm" where the old folks could have hills for company and where she could get to high school!

She started on again. The man in the car sat for a moment, looking after the slight girl walking up an empty, grass-grown road toward a lonely mountain.

Chapter 17

Cynthia Tears Down a House

The rusty tin mailbox marked "Bailey" at Brightwater Four Corners was watched as it had never been watched before in all the years it had sat there on a post. Every day on her way home from school, Cynthia tipped the lid eagerly. A week went by, and still no word from the county agent. Meanwhile, the girl's imagination had gone to work on Lem Matthews' land. She was building a house a little way below his cabin under two tall oak trees. On the outside, it was much like the Bee Tree Hollow house, except for the front door. That was painted green and had a shining brass knocker as "yeller as gold." The door had been lifted right off one of those new houses she had seen in Lincoln. Inside were two additions to the old furniture—a bookcase chock full of books and an electric washing machine. Cynthia had failed completely to heed Mr. Small's warning about letting her hopes rise high.

Saturday of the second week came. Still no letter lay in the mailbox. The girl began to wish she had been less in a hurry about dreaming up that new homeplace. After all, the ground under her house-with-the-green-door still belonged to Mr. Matthews. Then on the following Monday, there it lay in the bottom of the mailbox—a letter addressed to Miss Cynthia

Bailey. She slashed the envelope open, tearing the single sheet of paper in her haste. The few lines of writing read:

Dear Cynthia:
Lem Matthews has at last made up his mind. He doesn't want to sell any of his land. I'm mighty sorry, and I'll keep right on looking. It takes time to find a piece of good land nowadays.
Sincerely,
Amos Small

On the way home, the girl did a wrecking job. She tore down her house—green door, brass knocker, bookcase, washing machine, and all. There!

Now all at once, she noticed how bare and wintry the hollow had begun to look. The trees on Brushy, except for a few oaks, were leafless. The cut-over sides of the road had turned brown. The Branch, which now ran between brushless, treeless banks, seemed to mutter to itself like a lonely old person.

Arrived at the head of the hollow, Cynthia did not turn into the yard but went on up the trail through the pasture, past High Rock, and over the mountain's bald top. It was weeks since she had talked things over with Uncle Mose. Was he at home? Yes. A spiral of blue smoke rose from the trees that almost hid the tiny cabin.

Thud! Thud! He must be chopping wood. There he was. Why, he had cut down a sight of trees.

Who was that other man over yonder swinging an ax? She stared open-mouthed at the long-legged, slow-moving figure. It was her father! Uncle Mose and Pa were clearing a large, square space. They were clearing ground for a house.

Back over the top of the mountain went Cynthia. Down on High Rock she slumped. What to do now? What to do now? She sat and gazed out across the hollow and across Brightwater Valley without seeing a thing.

If only she had more time! Once her father had a place well started over there beside Mose, there would be no such thing as moving out beyond the mountains. A hawk screamed below her. Absently, she watched it rise higher and higher and circle farther and farther away until it was a speck. How clear the mountains were today! She could see the little notch which marked where Sourwood Gap was. The sight of that notch somehow comforted her. If there was a road through what looked from here like a solid mountain wall, might there not be some break in what seemed like a solid wall of difficulties?

That night the oil lamp in Cynthia's room burned after the rest of the cabin was dark. Hunched over the low washstand, she wrote and rewrote a letter—to Mr. James Holliday. The final draft read:

> Dear Mr. Holliday,
> Last summer you said that we'd find a new homeplace. Well, we haven't yet, and we never did get that money back. I went to look with Mr. Small for a little piece of land we could move our buildings onto but did not find one. Now Pa has begun to clear land on Brushy Mountain, and I'm worried to death. If we move up there, I'll never get to school again unless I leave home. Do you know about any bottomland we could buy and anybody to lend us some money to buy it?
> Yours Truly,
> Cynthia Bailey

A reply came promptly. It was a friendly letter, a kind letter. However, Jim Holliday couldn't do a conjuring act any more than the county agent could. He certainly would try to help her, he wrote, but it would take time. Couldn't she persuade her father to wait till spring about fixing up the place on the mountain? Maybe by then something could be found for them.

·

"Mose and I have got a right-smart patch cleared up on Brushy," Pa Bailey announced that evening as he smoked his after-dinner pipe by the kitchen stove. "If the weather stays fine, I can get a cellar dug 'fore Christmas."

Cynthia's brown head bobbed up as if jerked by a string. She stopped in the middle of working a problem in percentage to tackle an even harder problem than any in the book which lay in front of her on the kitchen table.

"Pa, why don't you try to find some bottomland somewhere 'fore you do any more up there? You could borrow money and buy it and pay back a little at a time."

At once Enoch Bailey was on the defensive. Never in his life had he borrowed a cent of money, and he didn't intend to begin now. Anyway, they were better off here than they would be out there among strangers.

The girl followed his glance toward the darkening wall of mountains and then back again to Brushy. She used to think that wall was a protection. Now it seemed to her a high hurdle which the Baileys must climb over. She shoved the book and pad of paper away from her and exploded:

"We wouldn't be better off in the woods than among strangers, not any of us. And I'd be miserable."

She began to talk about the past term at Brightwater School—how hard she was working to catch up with boys and girls of her own age. She didn't want to stop going to school next year, not for several years. Cynthia looked up to see both her father and her mother staring at her in amazement.

"Thought you hated school," said Pa.

"Not anymore I don't."

"You wants to go to high school?" asked Ma. She couldn't get used to the idea. None of her other children had gone any further than the Brightwater School could take them.

"I sure do. A girl needs more education now than girls did in the old days." She was repeating what the teacher had told her, though she didn't quite understand why this was so.

There was a long, troubled silence in the kitchen. Cynthia drew closer to the kerosene lamp on the table and tried to go on with arithmetic. She kept making mistakes, conscious that her mother watched her and that her pa was puffing away at his pipe like a steam engine. Presently, he took the pipe out of his mouth to say, "We'll have to find a way for you to git to school from up there." Then he thought of something to do at the barn.

Yes, I'll go to school along with the squirrels and coons and possums, thought the girl bitterly. If only there were more time—time for the county agent or Jim Holliday to find some land for them!

In a few days, Enoch Bailey began digging a cellar in the clearing up on Brushy. Cynthia wished it would pour rain so that he would have to stop. She would almost have welcomed a flood or earthquake. It was a relief when the winter rains did set in, even though the Hollow Road promptly turned into a red-brown river.

Somehow the girl got to school this winter—wading through puddles, splashing coat and dress with mud, slipping and slithering on muddy or sleety slopes to get around puddles. She went through rainstorms and ice storms and through cold winds which made her footing all the more precarious. Sometimes she rode on One-eye; more often she went on her own two feet. Only three days of the winter term did she miss—an all-time record for her. The after-school sessions with Miss Rogers grew longer. Sometimes Cynthia would come home to find supper on the table and her mother on the porch looking anxiously into the dusky-dark and listening for her step.

Chapter 18

A Big Time on Brightwater

The Brightwater School was ending with a "big time." Everybody who had been to the school in the past ten years was invited to a picnic—boys and girls who had moved away, boys and girls who had dropped out, and those who had gone on to high school. The youngest to receive an invitation was six-year-old Ellie Lou Bailey, and the oldest was Dessie Wheeler, who had a six-year-old daughter herself.

"Perhaps," Miss Rogers said, "we can have a Brightwater School reunion every year."

These words were crumbs of comfort to Cynthia, who was miserably unhappy. She couldn't bear the thought of this wonderful school year ending. Why, she might never even see Miss Rogers again! As chairman of the Committee on Arrangements, she helped the teacher write invitations and plan the picnic lunch, asking this one to fetch buns, and that one butter, and another cake, and so on. Miss Rogers was furnishing the hot dogs, and a friend of hers—a boyfriend, Cynthia suspected, and probably the same one who had given her that ring she'd worn lately on her left hand—was going to bring two whole gallons of ice cream.

On the evening before the great day, the Bee Tree Hollow

girl eyed every cloud suspiciously—even the cotton-wool ones. It mustn't rain! Then they would all have to crowd into the schoolhouse instead of eating under the pine trees in the schoolyard along the edge of the creek.

Next morning the sun rose over Turkey Hill into a sky that didn't show a cloud as big as a pocket handkerchief, and with it rose a gentle breeze. Everything would be perfect, thought the chairman, if two certain people were only coming. They had been invited. Unfortunately, Lincoln High was having a big time, too, on this same day. At least that was the reason Linda had given for their not coming. There was a baseball game, she wrote the teacher, and Paul was going to play. So was her boyfriend.

For weeks Cynthia had hoped that this picnic might mean a reunion and a making-up for the three of them. That was the reason she had worked so hard to finish the new dress she was wearing. It was a pink chambray with white collar and cuffs and a store-bought, white-leather belt. She and Ma had fussed and fussed to make it fit just right and hang perfectly. And when Cynthia tried it on, Ma had said, "Child, you're as pretty as a redbud bush."

She was the first one to arrive at the schoolyard. In a few minutes, Miss Rogers came walking up from her boarding place on lower Brightwater, looking, it seemed to Cynthia, prettier than ever before. There was such a happy expression on her face today.

Next came Mattie and the children from Spruceville. Cynthia did not recognize them when they rattled up in an old coupe. Then she heard Dan and Dave shouting, "Look where we are, Cynthy," and saw them waving from the rumble seat as proud and pleased as if in a gilded coach.

"Well, what do you think of it?" was the first thing Mattie said. "It's secondhand, but it looks almost new, don't you think?"

"Sure does," Cynthia agreed promptly.

"And now, I'm going to take Hattie up to Ma's for a little visit. I'll be back for the boys and Ellie Lou sometime after dinner. Don't you think I learned to drive quick?" she asked, starting the car with a self-conscious flourish. It bolted like a runaway horse and just missed landing in the creek.

The Wheelers hitchhiked and walked from their new home in Shady Valley. All six came, from Dessie down to Libbey, who had been to the Brightwater School for two years. Billy seemed to have forgotten that the world was coming to an end now that the family was settled in a new home. He wore his old smile that was as happy as a baby's.

Buddy Fuller and the little Fullers were there, in spite of the fact that tomorrow was moving day for them. "Ma said Minnie and I had to come home and help her as soon as we'd et our dinner," announced ten-year-old Sally. To the amazement of the chairman and everyone else, the two youngest Peters girls trudged down over Brushy Mountain. At first, in spite of cordial invitations from Cynthia and the teacher, they stayed on the edge of the little grove, perched on a boulder like two shy but inquisitive squirrels. Gradually, they edged closer and closer, first to watch the softball game, then to see the hot dogs roasting, and finally to accept proffered rolls and hot dogs for themselves. Cynthia suddenly felt sympathetic toward these girls. Maybe they, too, thought they were stupid, and maybe she would get to be as scared of people as they were if she went up on Brushy to live.

Now the teacher began to watch the Creek Road. "You don't reckon he's forgot, do you?" Cynthia asked when the last hot dogs were eaten and still no ice cream was even in sight.

"Oh no! He won't forget."

Even as she spoke, a black sedan rounded the bend in the road above the Wilson place. The two of them stood and watched to see who was in the car.

Cynthia of Bee Tree Hollow

"It's him," said Miss Rogers. Her face was alight with joy.

"Why that's Jim Holliday," Cynthia told her, as if he and Miss Rogers' friend couldn't possibly be one and the same person. "Wonder what he wants." She took it for granted that he had come to see her.

"Hello, Jim, our mouths are just watering," the teacher called cheerfully.

Cynthia saw the smiles that flashed back and forth between the young woman beside her and the man in the car, and she understood. The other children, too, who had trooped out to the road to witness the arrival of the ice cream, could add smiles and a ring and an engaged couple for the answer. "Teacher's a-going to marry him! Teacher's a-going to marry him!" they said to each other in loud whispers.

Cynthia turned away from the others so that no one could see her face. She pretended to be busy picking up scattered bits of paper. Jim Holliday engaged!

"I suppose," she told herself, "he's never thought of me as anything but a little girl, even if he did say one day I'd grown up." But he didn't have to pick out a girl yet, did he? She didn't want her Miss Rogers to get married yet, either. Why couldn't things ever stay the same for more than a few months at a time?

The Brightwater reunion broke up by mid afternoon, for all had come early, and several had a long way to go.

"Goodbye, Miss Rogers," said the Bee Tree Hollow girl gravely. "I'll never forget how you've helped me—never."

"Don't be so solemn. We're going to see lots more of each other. Anyway, you can't go home yet. Jim says he wants to take you and me to see a little farm over on Crabapple Creek. He's thinking of buying it."

"That's right," added the surveyor. "And I'm especially wanting your opinion of it."

This didn't make sense to Cynthia. Why did these two

invite her along when they went looking for a homeplace? She told Jim she was tired and that Ma wanted her to come home early, but he looked into her eyes and saw that she was making excuses.

"Come on, do your Uncle Jim a favor—just once. I'll whisk you over there and back in next to no time at all."

"All right."

Crabapple is a little creek which winds in and out among the hills between Brightwater and Spruceville. It drops suddenly down into the lower land all foamy and excited, then grows quiet and meanders along almost parallel with the Spruceville Road for a time before it joins Black Creek. The place Jim Holliday drove to today lay among low hills between the foamy part of the creek and the quiet part in the valley.

"There it is," he said, stopping the car and pointing to a small, neglected-looking farm back from the road between two folds in the hills. "Of course, the buildings are awful, but that's a mighty good piece of land. There's a nice little peach orchard back on the hillside, too. What do you think of it, Mary? And you, Cynthia? Do you like the place?"

They were what Pa Bailey would have called "sorry" buildings. The house was a plank-sided shack held up off the ground by a small pile of stones at each corner. Behind it, a little log cabin was falling to pieces. The barn leaned heavily to one side, too feeble to stand straight, and obviously leaky-roofed. The fences were tumbling down, and the gate into the weedy dooryard hung by one hinge. For a moment, Cynthia was amazed that Jim Holliday had brought them to see a miserable old farm like this. Then, all at once, this little cove among the hills called to her to come and live here. She felt a longing to have it—the sorry buildings and all—for her own homeplace.

She noticed the row of pines someone had planted long ago to shelter the cabin from winter winds, and the great-grandfather of a pine in front which shaded the stoop and strewed the yard with brown needles. There was no Brushy Mountain, but there was a low knob behind the house all covered over with laurel and rhododendron bushes. She could see Pa and Ma living here contentedly in their old home, rebuilt. If only the Baileys had discovered it before Jim Holliday had! She hoped hard that the teacher wouldn't like it.

"It's a lovely spot," said Miss Rogers.

"What do you think of it, Cynthia?" asked the surveyor. He had been watching the girl's face for several minutes.

Her blue eyes rested lovingly on the little hollow. "Seems like home."

He leaped out of the car. "I'll go and see if these folks want to sell. I heard they did."

A young man lounged on the stoop, whetting a scythe unhurriedly, as if only half pretending to use it. "Howdy! Ezra Williams, isn't it?" asked the surveyor.

"That's me. Come and set."

"I'm Jim Holliday. I work down at the dam, and I hear you're coming down to work there, too."

"Reckon so."

"We're sick of living in this hole," spoke up a young woman from the doorway. She sounded and even looked like Ella Bailey.

The two in the car sat quietly while the men talked on. Each seemed busy with her own thoughts. I suppose, thought Cynthia, she's planning just how she'll fix it all up fine-pretty here. She tried not to imagine the place as the Bailey home, but the picture kept rising before her eyes—the Bee Tree Hollow house made over and sitting there against the pines, her mother and father on the porch, Granny's flowers in the yard.

Jim Holliday came back to the car, taking quick, purposeful strides.

"Now, Cynthia," he began, "I want you to think hard and

fast. Would you and your folks like to live here? I know it looks pretty terrible now, but the land really is good, and it seems to me it could be made into a nice place. You could have electricity here, too." He pointed to the gleaming copper wires that followed the Crabapple Creek Road.

"Me? Us? But—But—"

"I know. I know you thought I wanted to buy it myself, but I didn't have any such idea. When I heard this fellow was coming down to work in Lincoln, I figured he might want to sell, and I thought right off of you folks. Remembered it was sort of pretty and quiet up here. Didn't want to get your hopes up before you'd seen the place, and before I knew for sure you could buy it. That's why I fooled you a little.

"Now, how about it? If you want the place, we'll have to grab it today, because Pete Corbett is talking about buying it. At least that's what Williams says. His price is eight hundred dollars."

She had to think fast, and she did it out loud. "It's exactly the kind of little cove in the hills we've been looking for. Of course, the house and barn don't seem fit to live in, but Pa wouldn't care about that. He wants to tear down our house and barn and even the fences and move them anyhow. He sure would like a nice little piece of bottomland like that. But how can he get here today to buy it?"

"He doesn't have to. I'll buy it and sell it to him for what I paid for it."

"Oh, that wouldn't do. Pa hates you like a rattlesnake—has ever since that day you knocked down his fence. If you offered him this whole country for eight hundred dollars, he'd be sure you were cheating him."

Jim laughed. "We'll get around that somehow. The next thing to do is buy it—and quick. I've got enough in my jeans to bind the bargain." He dashed back again to the man on the stoop.

Cynthia felt slightly dizzy as she walked back up Bee Tree Hollow late that afternoon. When she was a little girl, she used to grab hold of one of the porch posts at home and spin herself round and round it, faster and faster, until at last she dropped down on the doorstep, with the world reeling wildly about her. It would be several minutes before the mountains stood still again. This day reminded her of one of those spins.

Chapter 19

A Week of Suspense

Cynthia was out in the turnip patch cutting greens. At least, she was pretending to cut greens. Most of the time her eyes were on the two men who sat in the barn doorway. One was her father, the other a light-haired young man who was talking hard. In front of the barn stood a black sedan.

"O God, make Pa listen to him. Just make him!" she whispered as she stooped over the light green leaves.

They were standing up now. Was the visitor leaving so soon? He mustn't give up yet.

"Ma," she heard her father call, "we're going for a little ride."

What was the matter with Cynthia this morning? She cut off half a row of carrots instead of turnips. In the kitchen, she dropped things. She forgot to do what her mother asked her to do. "Git along out of my way," said Ma Bailey. "You're no more help than the cat."

In the yard, Granny hobbled about with the aid of a cane. "Cynthy, who's that man your Pa tuck off with? One of them railroad men?" she asked anxiously.

"No, no, Granny. That's Bud Simpson from North Fork."

The girl wandered about like a lost puppy—into the house

and out again, to the springhouse for a drink of water, to the barn and back. Piles of weathered boards and posts behind the barn brought her up short. Pa had been working fast these past few days! The smokehouse and the corn crib were down, and half the lumber lay loaded on a drag, ready for One-eye to haul it up Brushy. And yonder in the woods that cleared place waited. Was she too late with her little plan?

Long before a car could have gone even to lower Brightwater and back, the girl began to watch the road. "Come on, Lijer; come on, Bijer," she proposed suddenly. "We'll go up in the pasture."

Cynthia sat in the blazing sun for nearly all the summer morning, watching the deserted road. From here, she could see as far as Wheelers' mill, or rather where the mill used to be. The moment a black car came in sight, she started on a run down the hill. The hounds had to extend themselves to keep up with her. Cynthia arrived just in time to see Bud drive back down the hollow again and her father disappear into the barn.

"He wouldn't even stay and eat dinner," said Ma, disappointedly. All through the meal, the girl scanned her father's face, trying desperately to read his thoughts. He did not want to talk until he had finished his dinner and smoked his pipe. Every minute seemed like five.

Finally, he announced, "Bud and I went to Crabapple Creek to see a piece of bottomland over there. He thinks I'm a mighty good farmer, too good to be scratching seeds into a few inches of dirt on Brushy Mountain. He says a man like me oughter have land where he can raise a real crop." He threw back his stooped shoulders. There was pride in his voice.

In Ma Bailey's eyes, and in the set of her mouth, were only fear and suspicion. What was that Simpson boy trying to put over on them?

Enoch Bailey described the little, neglected farm—ten acres of good bottomland, pasture enough for a mule and two or three cows, a little peach orchard that only needed some pruning to make it bear well. And it was in a little hollow. A wistfulness had crept into his voice as he spoke.

He likes that place, thought Cynthia. "I could get to school from there," she said aloud.

"How's Bud figure we'll git money enough to buy any place?" Ma's voice was scornful.

Pa Bailey told them what Bud had suggested. He would buy the farm for eight hundred dollars, and the Baileys could lease it from him, move their buildings onto it, and, when they had paid the eight hundred dollars in rent, the place would be theirs. Of course, that was a heap of money to owe anybody, and he didn't know—

"We can manage," burst forth Cynthia. "I know we can. I'll work all my vacations and save everything I earn. I'll do anything. I'll—"

"We'll be better off on Brushy with Mose," interrupted her mother, who was still afraid of Bud and his offer and, for that matter, of everything and everybody beyond Sourwood Gap.

"But we'll not be better off, not if we can't raise enough to eat. Not if I can't ever go to school again. Not if we never see anybody but Uncle Mose—and the Peterses. Why don't we try it, Pa?" All her longing for a new kind of life was in her voice.

"I don't have to make up my mind yet. Bud's given me a week to think it over." He got up, knocked out his pipe, and took refuge from further argument in the barn.

Can I do it? Cynthia asked herself. Can I talk down his fears and Ma's? Well, she had six days. A lot of persuading could be done in that length of time. Long after the rest of the family was asleep, the girl lay in the darkness and thought.

It was amazing how many reasons Cynthia found during the next few days for being around the barn, in the fields, wherever her father was. She overfed the young chickens. She helped hoe the beans. And she talked! Also, she kept watch on that dragful of lumber behind the barn. As long as it just sat there, hope remained. The moment Pa hitched One-eye to it, she would know that her little plan had failed. And right along with that load would go her own bright hopes.

The girl knew better than to argue with her father. What she did was to keep harping on the possibilities of that farm in the hollow down on Crabapple Creek. How much land was there? What could he raise? How many peach trees in that orchard? And so on.

Now and then she referred to the subject of school—how hard it was to think that the Brightwater School was over, how much she had liked it since the new teacher came, and what a heap she had learned. Her father had little to say. His occasional comments, like "Is that a fact?" or "I reckon," gave her no idea whether she was making any progress.

"You talk about as much as your sister Ella," he said once, which meant, as Cynthia knew, that she was getting on his nerves.

The end of the week drew near. Cynthia felt discouraged. Her father appeared more and more doubtful about Bud Simpson's proposition. Her mother still had no desire even to ride over to see the place on Crabapple Creek.

She had to touch off the spark that would make them forget their fears. What was it? The answer to that question came on Friday morning, right in the middle of washing the breakfast dishes. They didn't know yet how much going to Crabapple Creek means to you, a voice inside her said. You haven't talked half enough about yourself.

Finishing the dishes in a hurry, Cynthia sought out her father in the hayfield. His back looked unapproachable. He kept right on swinging his scythe and appeared not to know she was there.

"Can I talk to you a minute, Pa?" she asked.

Her voice, something in her voice, compelled him to

turn around. Then he looked into her face, saw the desperate anxiety there, and could not go on with his work. Planting the scythe in the ground, he leaned on the handle and listened.

For the first time in her life, this girl really talked to her father about her inmost feelings—what the coming of Miss Rogers had meant to her, how she had gone through the cube root, how she had learned to write a good letter, how she had felt that day in the Lincoln library among all those books, and all the new ambitions and hopes the year had brought, and how they had grown stronger and stronger.

He was listening hard, with a little wonderment.

Cynthia began to repeat some of the nice things Miss Rogers had said about her. "She told me I'd done more work in one year than most girls do in three. She said a letter I wrote in school was good enough to send to the president of the United States."

The surprise growing in her father's face was anything but flattering.

"And what do you think Miss Rogers told me the last day of school? That I—Cynthia Bailey—was one of the smartest girls she'd ever known anywhere."

"The teacher done said that about you?"

"She sure did, and meant it, too. I know she did."

Later, she heard him repeating this compliment to her mother and saying, "She'd oughter have a chance." At dinner, he suggested they all drive over and take a look at that farm place on Crabapple Creek. To Cynthia's surprise, Ma was willing to go today.

"Now, Cynthy," said her father, when the three of them were sitting on the high seat of the wagon, "you tell your Ma point-blank what that teacher told you." As the girl talked, she saw a pleased look come into her mother's face. "Enoch," she said, "maybe this least child of ours is going to be a scholar."

The longest sixty seconds in Cynthia Bailey's entire life

were the full minute in which her mother sat and looked at the little farm on Crabapple without saying a word. Tensely, the girl watched the changing expressions on Ma's face—disapproval of the sorry-looking buildings and the weed-grown yard, a headshake at the rickety barn, then relief at the sight of wooded hills rising behind the snug hollow and enclosing it. Her face seemed to smooth out as she gazed at those dark mounds of earth and rock, as if they were the things that really mattered. At last—"I could be happy here," she said.

The girl suddenly realized that she had been holding her breath and let it out with a long sigh. "I could be happy here, too, and I could go to Spruceville High School."

I mustn't be sure yet, she told herself all the way home. Pa and Ma might change their minds overnight, and, of course, it must be what they wanted to do themselves. But it would be terrible to go to bed proud and happy over what she had accomplished only to wake up in the morning and find that the Baileys were going to live on Brushy Mountain after all.

Not till Saturday afternoon could she be sure. Even after her father had set out to meet Bud Simpson in Spruceville, Cynthia didn't quite dare to imagine herself living on Crabapple Creek. There still could be a slip. Pa could change his mind. So could Ezra Williams. So could Bud. Not till she had seen the written agreement between her father and Bud, not till she had read it twice over and read the names of the witnesses and noted the important-looking seal, could she quite believe that the Baileys had a new homeplace.

"We owes it all to Bud Simpson," said Pa Bailey. "Bud's been a real friend to us."

Cynthia's mouth twitched at the corners. She had to pick up Goldie, who dozed in her lap, and bury her face in the cat's yellow fur to stifle a giggle. How her father had come to hear of this place in the hollow must be kept a secret. He wouldn't like his new home nearly so well if he knew that his "interfering" daughter had found it for him with the help of that "skunk of a surveyor."

After supper, out came Pa's banjo for the first time in months. Once more the slopes of Brushy Mountain echoed to the old ballads he loved: "Barb'ry Allen," "The Little Mohee," "Sourwood Mountain." Presently, he struck up a livelier tune of his own, with words that came to him as he played:

> "We'll take our house and take our barn,
> Our mules and hound dogs, too—so!
> Over the mountains to Crabapple Creek
> The Baileys all will go, oh!"

"I'm right glad that place is in a little holler," murmured Ma Bailey.

Cynthia played with Lijer and Bijer and told them, "You're going to like Crabapple Creek. There must be a sight of squirrels and rabbits and coons back in those hills."

Next morning, she slept until long past her usual summer getting-up time. Nothing could disturb her today. Not since that airplane had droned over Brushy and the surveyors had stalked across the Bailey pasture had the girl known such peace. That terrible homeless feeling had gone—that feeling of not knowing where they would go when they had to leave Bee Tree Hollow.

Chapter 20

"Gee! You're Different!"

*"I got a girl at the head of the holler,
Hey-ho, diddle dum dey!"*

Cynthia jumped up from the bench by the springhouse. The bowlful of beans she had just shucked spilled all over the ground. Who was coming up the road singing that song? She actually thought for a moment that Paul Wilson was back.

*"She won't come, and I won't call her,
Hey-ho, diddle dum dey!"*

But it was Paul. Paul in his finest shirt, singing his loudest and waving his hand. He was riding with his father in a farm truck. There seemed to be a lot of old lumber in the back of it. Why were they coming here?

Ma Bailey ran to the kitchen door, took one look down the hollow, and said, "Lands!" Cynthia waved her hand, then waited, tense, to see what her father was going to say. Would he order the Wilsons off the place?

Enoch Bailey stood frozen in the path.

Matt Wilson swung down from the truck and called out in a hearty voice, "Howdy, everybody! Had to come back and see you folks and old Brushy once more."

"Howdy, Matt! Howdy, Paul!" Why, Pa was actually smiling.

"See what we're going to fetch home with us." The man beside the truck pointed to the load. "The old bell and the belfry. I've sure missed that bell. And I've got the porch posts, too. Going to build me a porch upstairs and down on the new house, just like the old one."

"Remember the little old seat in the yard, Cynthia, where we all wrote our initials that time?" put in Paul.

Did she!

"We're taking that along, too."

There was a beautiful light in the girl's face for a moment. Then she was grave again. "Why didn't Linda come, too?"

"Oh, she's gone on a picnic with her boyfriend."

Cynthia waited, but he added nothing. So, Linda hadn't even sent a message.

"How about a drink of that good cold spring water?" he asked. "And I want to drink it in the springhouse."

When he had drained the old gourd dipper twice, they sat down together on the bench outside. Left by themselves, they were constrained. How grownup Paul seemed! What could she talk about to this young man? For a few moments, he did not have anything to say. He was looking up at the bald, sunlit top of Brushy and across the valley to Turkey Hill. There was a mountain-hungry look in his eyes.

All at once, Paul began to ask her questions. Did they ever find that money? What were they going to do? He'd heard they were moving up on Brushy. Was that really true?

The girl's tongue was untied. There was so much to tell him! She talked fast, almost reliving the past year—all its suspense, the worry over Granny, what the girl had learned about herself from the new teacher, how desperate she had been when her father began clearing land on Brushy, and how at last she had found the place on Crabapple Creek and persuaded her father to lease it. And now she could—yes, she could go to high school!

Before the story was ended, Paul began to punctuate it with "You did?" and "You do?" and "Gee whiz!" When Cynthia stopped talking, she saw in his face complete amazement.

There was silence for a full minute. Then Paul burst forth, "Why, Cynthia, I had no idea—I thought you really wanted—" He stopped short. "Well, I might as well say it. I thought you didn't have a spark of ambition. You seemed like such a scared little kid; I couldn't see you ever doing anything but take to the tall timber with your pa and ma and stay there. But now you seem so different. And you're going to high school and going to work vacations to help pay for the new place. Gee! You are different!"

He was changed, too, she decided, still bright and full of fun but with a seriousness underneath she had never felt before.

"Cynthy! Cynthy!"

Oh dear! Ma wanted her. Just as she and Paul had begun catching up with each other! There was a heap more to tell him—what the new homeplace looked like, about the big time at the Brightwater School, and how they planned to have a school reunion every year. And she wanted to ask him dozens of questions.

"Cynthy! Come help me with dinner!"

Why must they go to work and cook a company dinner? That was what this early start meant. When you hadn't seen folks for a year, talking was more important than eating.

Ma Bailey thought just the opposite. "When you've lived as long as I have, child," she said, "you'll know that the best thing to do for company is feed them, especially when it's menfolks."

So the girl stayed in the kitchen while the chickens browned fragrantly in the skillet, biscuits and pies were popped in and out of the oven, and potatoes and turnips were peeled and boiled. Outside, Paul wandered restlessly about, playing with the hounds, stroking the cat, calling questions and remarks through the kitchen windows, and strolling up to the hickory tree and back.

Cynthia's idea that she and Paul would really "catch up with each other" today was a vain hope. By the time the dinner was cooked, eaten, and cleared away, and the dishes washed, the visitors had to start for home. The boy begged for one more gourdful of water, but the two only had a few moments together by the springhouse.

"Wish I'd known before what a bad time you were having," he told her gravely. "Sure hope things will go better for you now. You deserve a heap of luck, Cynthia, a whole heap."

"Thanks, Paul."

She stood under the holly trees in the yard and looked down the road long after the truck was hidden from sight. All at once, the old bell began ringing, as if someone pulled the rope in the belfry. To her, it seemed a voice out of the past.

Ding-dong. Fill up your basket quick. It's dinner time. Linda and Paul and she were racing down Turkey Hill with baskets of black walnuts. Yummy. Smell that shortcake.

Ding-dong. Happy birthday, Paul. Happy birthday. The little group was singing in the Wilson yard again.

Ding-dong. Now the sound came faintly to her ears, scarcely more than an echo. What was it saying? *Goodbye, Cynthia?* Or was it *See you again, Cynthia?* She wished she knew.

Chapter 21

A Task for a Family of Giants

Crack! Crack! The sound of boards thrown down in quick succession echoed back from Brushy Mountain like pistol shots. The noise was sweet music to Cynthia's ears. The place at the head of Bee Tree Hollow looked as if a hurricane had swept over it. Gone were the smokehouse, woodshed, and pigpen. A great gap was open in one side of the barn. Shingles, boards, beams, bricks, nails lay about in heaps. The litter-strewn yard was a beautiful sight to Cynthia. The Baileys were getting ready to move.

It was a task for a family of giants. They were not just moving out. They were lifting every movable thing off the old place—all the buildings, all the hay, the vegetables and fruits that were ready to pick, the shrubs and perennials in Granny's garden. Pa Bailey even planned to take down the silvery rail fences and pack them off down-creek. He'd dig up all of the trees and old rocks if he could, thought Cynthia.

The girl was in the kitchen with her mother. Their fingers moved swiftly as they cut up a bushel of green beans, packed them into glass jars, and set the jars to boil in the wash boiler. Now a loud whoa was followed by a howdy outside. It was Uncle Mose. He had been halfway up North Folk since sunup to borrow a mule to harness with One-eye. Without wasting a moment, he began backing the two mules up to the farm wagon he and Pa Bailey had loaded the day before. Presently, he was riding off down the hollow on the wagonload of hay. Summer was a busy season for Mose, with many hurry calls from Spruceville for his hand-carved "pretties." Yet he gave every day he possibly could to helping his brother.

"We're obliged to git everything out of this holler we kin while the weather's fine-pretty," Cynthia heard him say later in the day when he was back from Crabapple Creek. He had said the same thing before, but today she noticed anxiety in his voice. There was no time to lose. They all knew that by now. July was half over. In a short time, the huge gates of the dam would close. After that, the water would begin backing up in the rivers and branches. And nobody would be able to stop it or slow it down.

The girl saw that Uncle Mose and her father were staring at the sky above Brushy. The bald crest of the mountain stood out white against the leaden-colored bank of clouds. They went quickly back to work, not even stopping when Ma Bailey called, "Supper's on the table," and not stopping as long as they could see.

The rain mustn't come now, just when they needed a long stretch of fair days. It mustn't.

The rain did come. Cynthia woke about midnight that night to hear a persistent tapping on the roof. The tapping grew louder and turned into a heavy barrage. Splat—splat—splat sounded from the kitchen. Water was dripping through that leak in the roof. Goldie came mewing in through the window to dry herself on her mistress's bed. It was a long time before the girl went back to sleep.

In the morning, the storm had let up. Relieved, Cynthia went splashing gaily through the puddles. Cheerfully, she ate a big bowl of grits. Suddenly a sheet of liquid gray was let down between the kitchen window and the outdoors. It was like that all day, promising to clear up one minute, as if to fool people, then raining all the harder the next minute. There was nothing much to do but sit in the kitchen and watch it rain. Mr. Bailey sat about dumpily. Now and then he would go to the barn and putter around, then come back soaking wet to watch the rain again and dry off by the stove.

This went on for a week. In a few days, there was nothing left whatever to do but watch the yard turn into an expanse of mud and the road become a river. Ma Bailey and Cynthia could do no more canning because everything which had been picked was already canned. They had also packed up all the extra bed quilts and coverlets, bed linen, and the dishes which were not in use. Pa Bailey fussed around in the barn, heaping up tools and bits of junk. Then he, too, was out of a job.

***

The sun shone again. The Baileys sloshed hopefully about. There wasn't much they could do while everything was dripping wet and the road was bottomless mud. But at least the rain was over.

The long rain was not over. In two days, the skies were lead-colored again, and the relentless beating over the roof was heavier than ever. It seemed as if nothing could stop it now. This was a final deluge to wash away the earth.

"We'll be lucky to get out of here with the clothes on our backs," declared Ma gloomily when the second installment of rain had lasted for three days. "Listen!" In a lull between downpours, the girl and her mother sat silent. Little Bee Tree Branch was shouting, and that dull roar was Brightwater Creek.

Before she went to bed that night, Cynthia gathered together a little collection of special treasures. One by one she laid them out on the patchwork cover of her bed—a book of poetry Miss Rogers had sent her; a string of imitation pearl beads, which was a present from Ella on her sixteenth birthday; a bird Uncle Mose had carved for her; a handkerchief Linda had given her two years ago, so pretty that Cynthia had never used it; two dollars in pennies and silver earned by herself, picking and selling berries and ginseng; and a yellow newspaper clipping carefully pasted on a piece of cardboard. It was from the *Spruceville Record* and described that baseball game in which Paul had starred. Finally, she took her new pink dress down from a nail behind the door and added it and the white leather belt to the other precious things. Rummaging in the bureau for an old pillowcase, she thrust these favorite possessions into it, tied a string tightly around the top, and placed the lumpy bundle under her bed where she could grab it quickly, even in the middle of the night. She was ready if the Baileys once again should have to flee from a "big tide."

In the kitchen early next morning, she found that Ma, too, was packing up her treasures—a pink glass fruit dish given to her when she was married, and never used; a gold brooch and earrings set which had been her grandmother's; Sam's baby shoes; a tiny sweater worn by Ella, aged one year; and a lock of Cynthia's baby hair.

Pa Bailey was determined to save certain of his possessions, come "heck or high water." Heaped up on the barn floor lay a strange assortment of things. In the heap were his sharpest ax and his best hammer and saw, also useless keepsakes from long ago—an ox yoke; a tinkling string of sheep bells; the mold in which had been made, before he was born, the bricks for the chimney.

Chapter 22

A Wonderful Feeling

The rain stopped suddenly in the middle of the morning. The sun shone out so abruptly it made Cynthia blink. Within a half hour, Uncle Mose came slipping and sliding down the wet path. He and Pa Bailey sat on a bundle of hay in the dry end of the barn, talking gravely and shaking their heads while they waited for things to dry off.

Cynthia wandered about the muddy yard in the sun, as if let out of prison. Snatches of the talk in the barn floated to her ears somewhat like this: *week 'fore the road dries out—can't git up here with a heavy truck—after the dam closes—nobody 'round here now to borry a mule from—not fer all you was aiming to take nohow.*

Granny was out poking about. Leaning on a stout stick, she was going from one flower bed to another to see how much damage the rain had done. An invisible curtain seemed to be let down between her and the littered yard and the half-demolished barn. She did not sense what was going on. Whenever one of them tried to tell her about the new homeplace, the old lady either would not seem to hear or else would laugh mirthlessly, as though the person were cracking a poor joke. How in the world would they ever get her out of here, Cynthia wondered. Would they have to do it by force?

Cynthia of Bee Tree Hollow

"Cynthy! Cynthy!" she called. "Come help me fix this rosebush. The rain mighty nigh drownded it." She pointed with her cane to the little bush that grew under her bedroom window. It lay bent over with its roots half exposed.

The girl took the spade from Granny's hand, squatted down, and began scooping up the earth and filling in the washed-out place around the bush, "I'll fix it just fine," she said.

Clink! Her spade struck something hard. "There's a big old stone down there, Granny. I'll have to get that out."

It wasn't a stone. It was something metal. Deeper and deeper, faster and faster, Cynthia dug. Then, throwing down her spade, she began tearing away the earth with bare fingers, not even conscious of cutting herself on a sharp-edged stone. A flash like lightning had illuminated the past. It picked out old Granny here in the garden one rain-washed morning a year ago, bending anxiously over this same rosebush, patting, patting the earth around its roots.

The girl came running into the house, white-faced, shrieking— "Give me a knife. Give me a knife quick!" For a second, Mrs. Bailey thought Cynthia had gone out of her mind. She thought so, that is, until she saw what her daughter held in her hand—a rusty tin box. Then the dish she was wiping crashed onto the floor. "Give that to me!" she commanded. "You're so excited, you'll cut yourself, shore."

It seemed to Cynthia that she must scream, while her mother pried and whacked at the rusty cover. "Let me try! Let me try!" she begged.

Ma pried for ten minutes—they seemed like twenty. Then she spent at least five more trying to find the can of sewing machine oil. Finally, after another attack with the oilcan and knife, the rusty lid fell off. For a moment, neither the woman nor the girl could speak. There in the bottom of the box lay a roll of mildewed bills.

Ma Bailey counted them with shaking fingers. Cynthia counted them. They were all there—fifteen one-hundred-dollar bills.

"Thank God! Thank God! Thank God!" Mrs. Bailey repeated over and over, as if she were powerless to stop. When she did stop, she began to cry in her apron. Cynthia couldn't speak a word.

Granny, who had followed the girl into the kitchen, stared at the rusty box dazedly. Then, for an instant, light broke into her confused mind. "That—that's the money I hid when the Yankees was a-coming." She pondered, then added triumphantly, "And they didn't git it!"

"No, Granny, they didn't git it," repeated Cynthia, half laughing, half crying. She jumped up, hugged the old lady's thin shoulders, and kissed her on both cheeks. Pink spots came into the withered face where the girl's lips had pressed it. Granny smiled, well pleased with herself, then she said she was "plum tuckered out and was going to lay down."

Meanwhile, Mrs. Bailey was on her way to the barn, calling in a voice that Uncle Mose could have heard from his cabin. "Enoch! Enoch! We've found the money!"

Pa couldn't believe it until he had come and seen the precious wad of bills and counted them for himself. Why in thunderation had Granny gone and buried it, he wanted to know.

"She thought the Yankees were a-coming," said Cynthia. "Don't you remember she told you to bury the money? And when you didn't do it, she must have got up in the night and buried the box herself, and then marked the spot with that rosebush she'd just set out. And don't you remember, Ma, how her memory came back one day, and she tried to tell us something but couldn't talk so's we could understand? Poor, poor Granny!" She began to laugh hysterically. In a moment, her mother and father were both rocking with laughter, too.

Suddenly Ma looked sober and determined. "This time,

Enoch, you'd better put that money in the bank. I reckon even the Spruceville Bank is safer than this house with Granny in it." She seemed to have forgotten that cashing the check and hiding the money had been her own idea. Pa was too happy to remind her of it. "We won't have to live on somebody else's land now," he exulted. In ten minutes, he had One-eye caught and saddled and was splashing off to town.

It was the most wonderful feeling—like getting a windfall—to find fifteen hundred dollars buried in your own yard, fifteen hundred dollars you had given up forever! Cynthia couldn't make it seem true. She wanted to call her father back so that she could finger those hundred-dollar bills again and make sure they were real.

What couldn't they do now? They could pay for the place on Crabapple Creek and have electricity and buy a washing machine for Ma. She wouldn't have to work all her vacation time. When she did work, she could save the money she earned for all those extras a high school girl was bound to need.

Meanwhile, under her father's dusty black hat, an idea was forming as he surged One-eye down Brightwater. He, too, had plans for using some of that money.

It was past suppertime. Still Pa Bailey hadn't come home. He had been gone nearly all the long summer day. What could be keeping him? Cynthia and her mother kept going to the porch to look down the road. Dusk began to blur the outlines of the trees and shrubs. Still the road was empty. No, it wasn't. A stranger was coming. He was driving two black mules hitched to a wagon.

"Who you reckon that is?" Mrs. Bailey's voice was tense.

Cynthia had no idea.

"He'll be driving six black horses when he comes!" sang the man in the wagon.

"It's Pa! He's borrowed somebody's mules."

Slowly through the heavy mud drove Enoch Bailey, singing as he came. Behind plodded a somewhat dejected mule, tied to the backboard. It was One-eye.

"They're our own," he called out as he reined up proudly at the gate. "I bought 'em. They'll git us moved. They'll help me raise a crop over on Crabapple Creek."

When he had unharnessed the mules and eaten his supper, he had a job for Cynthia. "You write a better letter than I kin. I want you to set down and write to Bud that we've found the money and that I'm ready to buy the farm."

Cynthia wrote two letters. The second was to Jim Holliday to say:

We've found the money—all of it. Now we can pay for the place on Crabapple Creek.

Meanwhile, in the front bedroom, Granny lay with a smile on her lips and a look of peace in her tired old face. The Baileys found her the next morning lying still, with that same peace in her face. Sad as they felt, none of them could wish her back. They knew that Granny Bailey's life had ended just where she wanted it to—in Bee Tree Hollow.

Chapter 23

Uncle Mose Acts Mysterious

The head of Bee Tree Hollow looked as if an evacuating army had camped there. Gone was the cabin, except for the chimney. Gone were all the other buildings. The family lived in two small tents which Sam had brought up from Spruceville.

Hurry! Hurry! Hurry! The words seemed to be shouted into Cynthia's ears. She and Ma picked up the newly dug potatoes and put them into sacks while Pa and Uncle Mose loaded clapboards, beams, and posts onto the wagon. They worked these days from the time they could see their hands in the morning till they could no longer see them at night. They worked as if an invisible overseer stood with a great whip, driving them on.

Well they might! The gates of Lincoln Dam were closed. Brightwater Creek was rising. The water was nearly to the top of the high ledge above the swimming hole. Puddles grew bigger and bigger in the lower part of the schoolyard. Day after tomorrow, great trucks were coming from Lincoln to move the Baileys, but on account of the condition of the road, these trucks could get only as far as lower Brightwater. This meant hauling everything by mule team down the creek.

We'll have to leave a sight of this stuff behind, thought

Cynthia, straightening for a moment to ease her back and look around. And yet, what could they spare? Not the potatoes. Not the early apples which still hung on the trees. Not the jars of beans and tomatoes she and Ma had canned. Not any of next winter's food. They must have their furniture, too, and the rest of the lumber from the old buildings. She bent over and picked up potatoes faster than ever.

Everything had seemed to conspire to keep the Baileys in Bee Tree Hollow. First, the long rains had stopped short the work of tearing down the buildings. After that, for more than a week, the Hollow Road had been too muddy for carting heavy loads. Since then, there had been just too much to do in the time left, and too few people to do it.

Hurry! Hurry! Hurry! The rustling leaves, the talking brook, the roaring river in the valley—all seemed to say the same thing. And all the Baileys were hurrying this morning, all except Uncle Mose. What was the matter with him? Usually the fastest worker among them, he moved about like a snail and seemed to be doing more thinking than working.

"Kin I borry One-eye?" His voice broke the silence in the yard. "I've got some trafficking around to do."

Three people stopped working and stared at Uncle Mose. It didn't seem like him—not a bit like him—to go "trafficking around" now when they needed him so desperately.

"I need *you* more'n I need One-eye," said Pa Bailey bluntly.

The hunchback started at once for the pasture to catch the mule, seemingly unconscious of the despairing looks cast at his back.

"Hope he can't catch One-eye," said Cynthia to herself.

But Mose understood the stubborn mule as well as he did the creatures of the woods. He had apples and carrots in his pockets and knew how to use them. He talked softly into the mule's floppy ears and accompanied his remarks with gentle pats. Gradually, those ears, which had lain flat at the hunchback's approach, were raised. Presently, they tipped forward. In another moment, Uncle Mose was on One-eye's back and starting down the hollow at a fast clip.

"He won't get far. One-eye'll lie down with him, sure," Cynthia prophesied hopefully. Her hope did not come true.

Deserted by their one steady helper, the three Baileys worked on through the sultry hours, pausing now and then to wipe the sweat out of their eyes. At noon, they took out only time enough to eat cold fatback and cold beans and gulp down some buttermilk.

"Never in all my life had to work this-a-way in dog days before," said Ma Bailey grimly.

By midafternoon, Cynthia's back felt as if it couldn't be bent any more without actually breaking. Yet she kept right on bending it. And every now and then, a sharp knife seemed to be thrust under one of her shoulder blades. Still she worked on. There would be no letup for any of them until the hollow was in darkness.

Pa Bailey piled up the wagon to the almost-not-quite-toppling-over point, hitched the new mules to it, drove down to lower Brightwater, unloaded, came back, and started loading again. It was slow work for one man by himself. His face lengthened with the shadows. At four o'clock, he began counting the things they would have to leave behind—part of the hay, about half the lumber from the barn, those precious fence rails. They might not even get all the apples and peaches picked and carted down-creek.

Mose and One-eye were not seen again till late in the day. The hunchback wore a self-satisfied grin on his face and had the air of one who had accomplished some important secret mission. He was so cheerful the three tired workers at the head of the hollow could hardly bear his company.

"Oh, hesh up, Mose!" Pa Bailey told him when his brother had said for the third or fourth time, "We'll git everything out of here termorrer. Don't you worry."

Uncle Mose seemed immensely pleased, not only with himself but also with One-eye. "How much would you take fer that mule, Enoch?" he asked.

"You aiming to buy trouble? You know he's the orneriest, balkiest mule in the country, don't you?"

"Not with me, he ain't. He and I are buddies."

For the first time that hectic day, Pa Bailey grinned. "If you can git him up over the mountain, he's yours," he said skeptically.

Cynthia, like her father, was ready to bet cash-money that the old mule would never climb Brushy to his new owner's cabin. Again she guessed wrong. Mose swung lightly onto the mule's back, said, "Git along, Buddy," and off he went, calling over his shoulder that he would be down in the morning as soon as he could see to get there.

One-eye is wiser than we ever supposed, Cynthia decided. He had sized up Uncle Mose just as the wild things did—an old softie who would make a pet of any animal.

Hurry! Hurry! Hurry! Even the darkness did not end the labors of the Bailey family. Out in the garden, Cynthia and her mother worked by the narrow light of a lantern, digging up the precious rose bushes, the snowball bush, the bleeding hearts, and the verbenas and putting them into pots for the journey tomorrow.

Another lantern threw moving paths of light and long-legged shadows about the yard as Pa Bailey finished putting the last load on the wagon.

Was there ever such a moving!

Chapter 24

The "Working"

One day more! One day more! Brightwater Creek seemed to roar the warning through the valley when Cynthia woke up the next morning. The Baileys had till noon today to get everything they could carted down-creek and ready for the big trucks from Lincoln. Early tomorrow morning, they must take leave themselves with all the last things. To delay longer meant to risk being trapped at the head of the hollow.

Uncle Mose was better than his word. He appeared out of the woods before he could see, except by the swinging light of a lantern, and offered to drive the first mule load down-creek. There was nothing slow about him this morning. He ran around like a boy, catching mules and harnessing them and driving off down the hollow before the last bats had flown home. His voice floated back through the thick mist as he sang cheerfully:

> *"Chicken crowing on Sourwood Mountain,*
> *Hey ho, diddle dum dey!*
> *Git your dogs, and we'll go hunting,*
> *Hey-ho, diddle dum dey!"*

"A body would think he was happy over our leaving,"

Cynthia said to herself disgustedly. However, she had little time to bother about her uncle or anybody else. As soon as she could see which were leaves and which were fruit, the girl was up on a ladder picking apples.

Some time later, as she was about to move the ladder to another limb, she glanced down the road. "Lookee yonder!" her voice rang out across the clearing, like a sudden burst of song. The ladder crashed to the ground as the girl took a flying leap. A small black car was rattling up the road, and in it were Sam, Mattie, and the children.

"How'd you git off on a working day to come?" Mr. Bailey wanted to know.

"Told the boss that my pappy'd be drowned if I didn't git up here and help. Now, what do you want me to do first?"

Mrs. Bailey did wish she'd known about their coming in advance, for she hadn't a thing left "fitten for them to eat."

At that moment, Dan and Dave lifted down from the rumble seat a clothes basket covered over with a white cloth and proudly staggered over with it. "It's chock full of food," they chorused.

Ma stopped worrying.

"We brought enough for everybody, but the Wheelers will likely bring a lot of victuals, too," Mattie said.

"The Wheelers?" Cynthia and her father and mother shouted all at once.

"Didn't Uncle Mose tell you they was coming?"

At that moment, a loud rattling was heard on the road, and another jalopy lurched around the bend. It was Lem Wheeler and three of his boys, come all the way from the head of Shady Valley. "Us Brightwater folks will always be neighbors, no matter how many dams they build," declared the miller. "That's what I told Mose yesterday when I saw him in Spruceville."

So this was what Uncle Mose was so happy about. He had planned a "working" as a surprise.

Suddenly the weight was gone from the girl's shoulders. For days she had felt as if she carried an actual load there. Now her shoulders were light again.

"Any more coming?" asked Enoch Bailey.

The visitors smiled.

The Baileys didn't have long to wait for the answer. In fifteen minutes, the Wilson truck joined the other two cars by the gate.

"Here I am, Matt Wilson—light trucker and mover," he called out. "I'll keep this machine rolling up- and down-creek all morning."

Cynthia almost pitched off the ladder, trying to see if Paul were not in that truck somewhere. No, he hadn't come.

It was really enough to make anybody dizzy to see such a lot happening all at one time in one place. Cynthia and Billy Wheeler picked apples. Mattie and Ma packed kettles and pots and pans and clothing. Matt Wilson and Pa loaded a truckful of timber. The two other Wheeler boys piled up more lumber ready for the next load. Everybody worked, even little Ellie Lou Bailey. She ran errands, fetching this and that—a box to put nails in, empty baskets for the apple pickers, gourds dripping with ice-cold water from the spring for the men.

The only ones who had nothing to do but get in the way were the hounds Lijer and Bijer, and they felt so out of things they soon took to the woods.

Best of all, everybody was singing or whistling or joking. "A body'd think we was at a play-party," said Ma, her eyes as sparkly as a girl's.

Soon the Wilson truck was full of lumber and was rolling down the hollow.

Now Mose came back with the mule team, looking like a magician who has just pulled a white rabbit out of his hat.

At sight of him, Cynthia ran across the yard, threw her arms around his neck, and kissed his brown, bristly cheek.

Mose's face crinkled up till his eyes were bright slits and his face one wide smile.

"Cynthy, you ain't give me one of them bear hugs since you was the size of Ellie Lou."

"You can have a hundred."

The afternoon was like a calm after a tornado. The Wheelers left as soon as they had eaten dinner. Mr. Wilson was off for home early with his truck full of things to leave at Crabapple Creek on his way. "I'll be back early in the morning if I can get through the mud holes," he told the Baileys. They did hope he could make it, for there was certainly at least one more truckful of lumber in the yard, and more potatoes and apples than the wagon could hold.

Luckily, the weather was just fine that night. As Ma Bailey said, "They would have been soaked through if a thunderstorm had bust loose." Uncle Mose didn't bother to go back home but rolled up in a blanket on the ground. Sam and Mattie stayed, too. Cynthia gave up her tent to them. She and Ellie Lou slept under the sky upon a heap of hay left on the floor of the old barn. Dan and Dave gleefully carried blankets up on the side of Brushy and imagined they were camping miles away in a deep forest. The dogs joined the boys on the mountain. Goldie, with a *pr-rup* of joy, inserted herself between Cynthia and Ellie Lou.

Cynthia lay and watched the stars swing slowly across the wide dark space between Turkey Hill and Brushy Mountain. It was some time before she settled down for her last night's sleep in Bee Tree Hollow.

Chapter 25

Goodbye, Bee Tree Hollow

It's here! thought Cynthia the moment she woke up. *That day I've thought about for more than two years. That day I've dreaded some of the time and wished for some of the time. It's here. It's today! In a few hours, I'll be leaving Bee Tree Hollow forever.*

The only sign of morning was a faint lessening of the darkness over Turkey Hill. Yet lights were already moving back and forth across the yard. Loud squawking broke the silence as Uncle Mose and Sam struggled to catch the hens and put them into coops and boxes for the trip to their new home. Now the smell of coffee was mingled with the smell of wood-smoke. Ma Bailey and Mattie were cooking breakfast.

Rubbing her eyes and yawning, Cynthia jumped up, ran a comb hurriedly through her hair, smoothed the creases out of her old cotton dress, and was ready for the big day. Tomorrow, nobody was going to make her get up early, nor the day after tomorrow, nor the day after that.

She ate breakfast perched on a stone in the yard. The last chair was already on the wagon, along with the hens. Anyway, she was too excited to care what she ate or where she ate it. The boys came whooping down from the woods with the hounds barking at their heels.

By seven o'clock, Matt Wilson was back with his truck for one more load. "Water's over the Brightwater Road in one spot and rising fast," he reported. "I'll have to fill this up and git right along. And you folks must be out of here in a couple of hours if you don't want to git stuck."

They darted like water spiders back and forth from the piles of things left in the yard to the truck. The men and boys demolished the woodpile and threw it into the truck with almost the speed of a steam shovel. They topped the load with sacks of apples and potatoes, and Mr. Wilson was off again.

In another hour, Sam and his family left. They wanted to get their car through that bad place in the road before the water rose any higher. What did Uncle Mose whisper to them before they left? Cynthia wondered. She had seen him whisper like that to the Wheelers, too.

The three Baileys and Mose were left alone, feeling a little like people marooned on an island. Cynthia and her mother went to work on all those innumerable "last things." They packed up the cups and plates used for breakfast, the old black coffee pot, the hominy kettle, and the drinking gourd that had hung for years in the springhouse. They gathered together the swill buckets, the wood box, the broom, and the mop. They poured water over the remains of their last fire in Bee Tree Hollow.

"Can't get nary another thing on that wagon now," Pa Bailey and Mose agreed finally. But nothing had to be left except the fence rails and a few apples. The moving bee had done its work well.

"Come on! Let's git started!"

Ma and Cynthia thought they were ready till Ma spied the herb bed. She'd forgotten to dig up the sage and the mint. Then, just as they were about to climb up on the wagon seat again, two hens appeared which had somehow missed the general hen roundup in the morning. It took twenty minutes to run them down and get them into a sack.

Next, the men decided the load had to be tied down. Where in blazes was that piece of rope? It had been right here a minute ago. Ten more precious minutes were spent hunting for the missing rope, which all the time was hanging from the tailboard.

They were off! Ma had the herbs in her lap. Cynthia held Goldie in a basket.

"Giddap!" said Pa Bailey.

"Whoa!" yelled Cynthia. "Where are Lijer and Bijer?"

The hounds had been underfoot since morning, but now they were nowhere to be seen. They all whistled and called. Cynthia looked under the lilac bushes where the dogs loved to lie on warm days. A baying sounded from halfway up Brushy.

"Drat the fool hound dogs! They've gone and treed a squirrel," said Mose.

Whistling and calling were of no use. Cynthia had to climb clear up above the hickory tree and drag them by their collars, hoist them up on the top of the overloaded wagon, and hold them down. She wished she could make them understand that there were squirrels where they were going.

"Giddap!" shouted Pa Bailey once more. The mules started. The wagon creaked under the load. They were off. Cynthia and her father and mother sat on the seat. Uncle Mose perched on top of the load, holding one end of a rope. At the other end, Jumping Jane tugged and hung back, unwilling to leave her old pasture.

Out of the corners of her eyes, Cynthia could see that her mother kept turning to look around and that tears were running down her cheeks. As for herself, she kept her eyes fixed on Sourwood Gap, refusing to look back at her old home or down at the ghosts of homes—the lone chimneys standing where cabins used to be—the gaping cellar holes. Above the rushing waters of Brightwater, the little church gleamed white through the trees. It was safe. Scattered Brightwater folks would come back every year to put flowers on the graves behind it, and Granny would sleep there undisturbed.

Halfway down Brightwater, she turned for one quick glimpse of Brushy and of High Rock. The mountain would still stand up there against the sky after the hollow had become a lake. High Rock would welcome her when someday she came again up the other side of the mountain to sit on the moss-cushioned seat and dream back old days.

She was thinking now not of the old days but of the new days ahead. They could be happy in that little cove, she knew. She had learned something in these hectic days of moving. A home couldn't be picked up and moved, not if you carried with you every stick and stone and every flower in the garden. Home was a feeling inside you, and you could take that all over the world. A pleasant sound issued from the basket in her lap. She lifted the cover a crack and peered in. The yellow cat, who had been lost and uneasy ever since the Baileys started tearing down the house, was purring contentedly.

Chapter 26

Welcome to Crabapple Creek

The black mules plodded along under the blazing sun with their ears laid back. Their flanks were dark with sweat. The three people on the wagon seat did not talk anymore. They were thirsty and hungry—terribly hungry. In the excitement of leaving, no one had thought of bringing along anything to eat or drink. And there would be nothing to eat over there until the stove was set up and a fire started and the dishes unpacked, thought Cynthia. She sighed as she pictured all the work and confusion waiting for them at the end of this hot, jolting ride.

They must be nearly down to the turn-off now. From there it was less than a mile to their new home. Would that little cove in the hills look as pleasant today as it had when she saw it last? The wagon creaked and lurched. Mose was making a sharp turn. Here it was—the winding dirt road. Now they were climbing that long hill. Here was the last bend in the road!

Ma leaned way forward, trying to catch a glimpse of the place before the slow mules could get there.

Suddenly the hounds, which had been trotting dejectedly beside the wagon, bounded ahead, barking in wild excitement. Why, where did all those cars come from? There were six parked beside the barn and along the fence! And who were those people running around in the yard? You could hardly see what the place looked like with so many people all over it. Cynthia strained her eyes to recognize the moving figures before she was near enough to see anything but vague shapes and splotches.

"Who-all are they, Uncle Mose? And what are they doing here?"

Mose grinned. "You've had a working over yonder. Reckon now you've got a working here."

Smoke rose from a fire in the yard, and figures bent over it. They were cooking—cooking dinner. Hands and hats began to wave. Cynthia and her mother waved back without knowing to whom they were waving. A woman in a bright blue dress with an elaborate hairdo ran out to the road.

"Well, if it ain't Ella!" exclaimed Ma Bailey. "All fixed up like a picture out of the newspaper."

That figure propping himself against the barn door was Joe, of course. And that human semaphore was a dark-haired boy waving both arms. It was Paul Wilson!

Now a slender girl detached herself from the group around the fire and flew down the road to meet them. At the sight of her, Cynthia made Mose stop and let her down. The two girls ran into each other's arms.

"Linda!"

"Oh, Cynthia, how I've missed you!"

"And I've missed you—terribly."

"We'll see each other often now, won't we?"

"Oh yes. Let's never again be away from each other so long!"

Paul just said, "Hi, Cynthia," grinned, and began helping the men unload the wagon.

"How are you, Cynthia?" It was a pleasant voice, a familiar voice, and it reminded the girl from Bee Tree Hollow of arithmetic. Yes, the schoolteacher, Miss Rogers, was here. Only she was Mrs. Holliday now. And here was Mrs. Wilson. She seemed to be in charge of the dinner-getting, but she left the fire long enough to clasp Mrs. Bailey's hand and give Cynthia a hug.

And here were Sam and Mattie and the children and all the Wheelers.

Now a strange sight met the girl's eyes. Her father held one end of a table and Jim Holliday the other as they carried it out under the pines.

"Mary, you and Cynthy sit down and rest yourselves," said Mrs. Wilson, bustling back to the fire. "We're going to take dinner right up."

"Lookee!" cried Cynthia. "They've moved the furniture in." While some of their old friends had been moving them out of Bee Tree Hollow, these others had been working here yesterday and all this morning, moving them in. Already the two-room shack looked home-like. Chairs and tables were placed in the rooms. The beds were not only set up, they were all made, ready to sleep in, with some of Mrs. Bailey's prettiest coverlets on top. In the kitchen, Paul and his father were setting up the stove, and Ella and Mrs. Holliday had begun unpacking dishes.

Outside, others were moving the rest of the furniture into the barn, where it would be stored until the new house was ready. Still others were sorting out the lumber and stacking it handy for use.

"What do you think of this gang?" Paul asked her in the kitchen. Not waiting for her answer, he dashed off to help in the yard.

The girl looked across the littered yard, over the roof of the shack, and pictured the place the way it would look when the shack was gone and the Bee Tree Hollow cabin stood back there in the pines with the same old flowers and shrubs around it.

Ma Bailey gave a sudden exclamation and hurried to where overgrown shrubbery was intertwined in an unkempt mass. "There's a little old moss rosebush here, sure enough," she called delightedly. "And white lilacs, too!"

How good that first dinner on Crabapple Creek tasted! For days Cynthia had scarcely known what she ate. Now she could really stop to enjoy a meal, for the Baileys were moved—not only moved, but partly settled.

The animals, after eating their first dinner here, seemed reconciled to the change. The hounds stopped sniffing suspiciously at everyone and everything and went to sleep on the cool pine needles. Goldie jumped upon Cynthia's lap and turned into a purring yellow ball. Jumping Jane was already having fun looking for a weak spot in the pasture fence.

Anyone watching Cynthia's movements after dinner would have seen her stroll casually about the yard for a few minutes as if she were going nowhere at all, then disappear into the old barn. Within waited Pa and Ella and Joe, who had also entered the place with elaborate casualness.

"They brung it—the washing machine," whispered Pa. "It's over there." He pointed to a hump in the Bee Tree Hollow hay heaped up in the mow.

Still talking in whispers, they made their plans. They would keep the wonderful machine hidden out here until the house was ready to live in and the wires which sung in the breeze were carrying electricity. Then Ma would be invited to visit Ella and Joe, and when she came home, the house would be all lighted up, and the clothes would be slosh-sloshing in the white washer.

The girl looked as if the lights had been turned on already—right behind her eyes. She had had to talk herself hoarse to Pa, but her plan to take some of the money left over after buying this place and have electric lights and a washing machine for her mother was going to come true!

The cars drove away. Before dusk, the settling party was over. Only one visitor stayed on—Uncle Mose. Mose wanted to take a hand with Pa Bailey when he patched the barn roof tomorrow so that the things stored in the barn wouldn't get wet if a shower came up suddenly.

Linda and Paul climbed reluctantly onto the truck with their father and mother. "Cynthia, you've got to promise to come down and stay at our house right soon," said Linda.

"You bet you have!" added Paul.

Cynthia promised.

"Child," said Uncle Mose that evening, "you looks like your old self again—happy and purty."

The girl sat watching him whittle a rabbit out of a chunk of wood. The hunchback always had to be whittling. "Only you've been growing up so fast lately, I can't call you 'child' nor 'little Cynthy' no more."

At these words, the girl looked still happier and "purtier."

"Look!" She pointed suddenly to a star which had pricked through the pink glow beyond the hills. "That's the same star we used to see over Brushy."

"It's follered you over here. Reckon a sight of other good things has follered you, too."

Chapter 27

"You Don't Act Afraid"

Cynthia was taking the longest time to get dressed this morning. She was stepping into her new plaid skirt and pulling on the blue sweater which she had somehow managed to knit this frenzied summer. She was sticking a bobby pin here and a comb there to make her fly-away hair stay just where it should. Now, standing up in a chair, she surveyed as much of herself as possible in the small mirror on the wall. Yes, the skirt hung evenly. Those blue bobby socks just matched her sweater. And her saddle shoes were new and bright.

Did she look like other high school girls? Or was she still little Cynthy from way back up in Bee Tree Holler? A glance at her legs in the glass told her one thing—at least, no one could call her "little" anymore. She was tall.

It was the hardest work to swallow breakfast. The smallest spoonfuls of oatmeal seemed like enormous lumps. They had to be fairly pushed down her throat. Her stomach had felt strange when she got up. Every bite of food made it feel stranger.

There was no sense in hurrying. It wasn't seven o'clock yet, and the bus didn't leave the corner till quarter of eight. Yet the girl dashed off down the road as soon as the last mouthful of oatmeal was eaten. Perhaps the clock was wrong, even though it had been set yesterday by the mailman's watch. Perhaps the bus driver's watch would be fast. Anyway, she couldn't sit still or even walk. She had to run.

This was the day Cynthia had thought about for nearly a year and had planned for ever since Pa Bailey had decided to move to Crabapple Creek. This was her first day at Spruceville High School. And now that it had come, the girl was scared stiff. She was like an actress who gets a part in a play and studies that part for weeks, only to be struck dumb with stage fright on the opening night. Shame alone kept Cynthia from turning around and beating a retreat up the home road.

Instead, she sat down forlornly on a rock at the corner of the Spruceville Road and waited. The longer she waited, the bigger her fears grew of this big school where she did not know a soul.

"H-h-howdy."

A weak voice sounded behind Cynthia. She jerked her head around to see a girl standing almost at her elbow. This girl was small, with shoulders that drooped. She wore a badly made dress which was a size too large. Her face would have been pretty if it had not been so thin and filled with worry. Why, thought Cynthia, this girl is me as I used to be. I looked like that two years ago.

"Hi, there!" she said. "I'm Cynthia Bailey, and I live up yonder on Crabapple. Who are you?"

"Ellen Tilbury. I lives yonder." She pointed down the Crabapple Creek Road in the opposite direction from the way Cynthia had come. "We just moved here this summer. Had to. Our old homeplace is all under water now."

She seemed to feel some kind of bond between herself and this tall, strange girl and, without another word of encouragement, began to pour out an account of the past year. It was a story in many respects like Cynthia's own, except that Ellen was the oldest of a family of children, instead of the youngest. Also, she had not been lucky enough to have friends like Miss Rogers and Jim Holliday to encourage her.

"And now," went on the small girl, "I have to go to Spruceville High, and I don't know nobody in the whole school, and I wish I'd stayed at home!"

"Oh, yes, you do know somebody," broke in Cynthia. "You know me. I'm going to Spruceville, too, and you're the only person I know in the whole school. So don't you dare run back home and leave me."

At that moment a yellow bus came around the corner. Grasping Ellen firmly by the arm, the other girl fairly pushed her onto the bus and into a seat. The small one looked up at her in awed admiration.

"You don't act one bit afraid! I reckon it takes a heap to scare you."

The bus quickly filled up with boys and girls. They all seemed to know one another, and none of them were freshmen. At least, so it seemed to the two from the Crabapple Creek Road. It was the same way when they climbed down in front of the brick schoolhouse.

"Hi, Buddy!" "Hi, Mary!" "Lookit, here comes Anne!" "How's Pete?" The joyous greetings floated over and around them but never were directed towards them.

"Come on, Ellen, I'll show you over the schoolhouse," said Cynthia, quite as if she were a guide instead of a girl who had never set foot inside the building herself.

That was the way the whole day went. Nobody suspected that the tall, pretty girl in the blue sweater and blue socks was playing a part. The little one with her—she was scared all right, but the other one knew her way around, or so it seemed. How little any of these boys and girls understood this girl from Bee Tree Hollow and the frightening, bewildering changes this day was bringing to her!

Once, she somehow got into the wrong classroom with a bunch of seniors. They all laughed when she discovered her mistake and ran out of the room. Again one of the teachers, who was nearsighted, turned thick, shiny glasses toward her, frowned, and asked a question. Cynthia was completely tongue-tied, though she had the answer, too late.

Yet, along with these experiences came pleasant adventures, too. And friendships of Bee Tree Hollow days stood her in good stead. At recess, a sophomore came running up to ask, "Aren't you Linda Wilson's friend, Cynthia? She told me to watch out for you."

And after class, that nearsighted, cross-looking teacher had called her back as she was leaving the room, smiled sweetly, and said, "Mrs. Holliday has told me all about you and how you've been working overtime at school. When you strike any snags here, come to me, and I'll help you if I can."

Ellen Tilbury followed Cynthia about all day like a small, pale shadow, acting as if she couldn't possibly make a mistake if she did exactly what her new friend did. "It was all strange to you, too. And you'd never been to anything but a little bit of a school either. But you didn't act scared," she told Cynthia again as they were riding home on the bus.

Now for a moment, as they rolled over the top of White Ledge Hill, Cynthia had a glimpse of that blue mountain wall with the notch in it. Then the bus sped downward and the wall was gone, obscured by lower but nearer hills. She felt today like laughing at the Cynthia Bailey who thought that everything on this side of the mountains was unfriendly and different. Why, it was all the same everywhere, whichever side of the mountains you lived on.

"Goodbye, Ellen."

"Goodbye, Cynthia. See you tomorrow."

"Sure will."

They separated.

Even before Cynthia came in sight of home, she could hear the *rat-a-tat-tat* of hammers. Under the pine trees behind the shack, the new house was rising fast from the wreckage of the old house that had stood in Bee Tree Hollow.

Chapter 28

Everything is Different

"But it's beautiful—actually beautiful here!"

Cynthia could hardly believe she was seeing aright. Here they were again—she and Linda and Paul—standing on the side of Buzzard Mountain looking down into "the big hole." Only there was no hole, no ugly red crater. Below them stretched a serene lake, soft blue like the April sky overhead, dotted by wooded islands, which were really the tops of hills.

"That one's Whitetop. I remember the white rock right on the top of it," said Paul.

"Yes, and the little knobby one with dogwood all over it is Possum Hill," added Linda.

It was a game, picking out the old landmarks in a place that looked new-created today. Over there was Joy's Peak, the scars in its quarried sides all hidden by water. Here, where the gravel pit had been, and beyond, where an enormous cement mixer had stood, all was green with newly planted shrubs and seedling trees.

How quiet it was! No more thunderous blasts. No more screeching and creaking of machinery tore the silence of the hills to pieces.

The noise was in the powerhouse. Yet this dull roar was different. It was rhythmic and subdued.

"Like deep-voiced giants muffled and singing together," said Cynthia.

"The giants that used to live in the river." This was Paul. He was having the time of his life today, inspecting the walls of the dam, the sluiceway, the giant turbines in the powerhouse, and every bit of the shining machinery there, and asking questions of the chief engineer. Paul was studying engineering now down at the state university, and every mechanical detail of this place fascinated him more than ever before. Hardly could he be persuaded to sit down under the trees by the reservoir and eat the lunch Linda and Cynthia had brought.

For Cynthia, this was the best part of the day, sitting here at the water's edge, watching white cloud reflections drift across the blue lake. She grew suddenly thoughtful. What had happened here was for all the world like what had happened to her. Back there under Brushy Mountain, she had run wild, doing what she pleased when she pleased. Then the quiet life had been all torn up. It seemed as if everything she loved was being blown to bits as violently as these hills were dynamited. Now, like the river, life had smoothed out again, and widened and deepened, too.

"Hey! What are you so solemn about, Cynthia?" cried Paul. "This is a picnic."

"What are you studying out?" Linda wanted to know.

The other girl smiled. "Only how different everything is from two years ago." She told her thoughts about the river, not expecting they would understand.

"Yes," said Linda, "that's exactly how it has been with us, too. Were we homesick last year!"

"You and Paul—homesick!" It didn't seem possible.

"Gee whiz!" Paul exploded. "We all were. It was months before that new place seemed like home."

"And then going to a school where we didn't know anybody at all—wasn't that something!" added Linda.

Why, they felt the same way I did, thought Cynthia. She told them about her first day at Spruceville High—how big that brick building had looked—and what a mob two hundred boys and girls and five teachers had seemed. Now she thought Spruceville High was wonderful.

Later that afternoon, Paul drove Cynthia back home to Crabapple Creek. What did he think, the girl asked. She might be graduating the same year as Linda did. Two of the teachers had offered to tutor her summers so that she could do the four years' work in three. If she did that, she reckoned nobody could call her stupid again.

"Stupid! You!" Paul fairly exploded. "Anybody that ever called you stupid was stupid himself."

He talked about the past year at the university and about his own plans. He didn't mind admitting that he had wanted to take the next train back home that day last September when he arrived in Dicksville. Well, that was last fall. Now he was on the basketball team and in the band and knew a lot of fellows. He'd probably hate like everything to leave Dicksville when graduation time came. And yet he was keen to tackle a job of engineering.

The boy fell silent, watching for the turnoff. Then, as they started up the Crabapple Creek Road, he began to talk almost breathlessly as if there were certain things he must get said before reaching the Bailey place.

"When I settle down, it won't be in any old city, and it won't be down in the level country, either. A lot is going to be happening right around here, and Paul Wilson will be right in on those doings. Someday I'll be the big boss on a job like building Lincoln Dam."

Neither spoke for a few minutes. Both, as they soon discovered when Paul went on, had been thinking about the same things.

"Someday, too, I'm going to build me a house in a little cove in the mountains. And it will look a heap like our old house in Brightwater, and yet be as up-to-date as one of those new Lincoln houses."

"Will it have a green door and a knocker as shiny and yellow as gold?" asked Cynthia, with a laugh at the recollection of her own dream house.

"Sure will—if that's the way you want it!"

They smiled at each other but had to leave it at that today; for, at this moment, Uncle Mose hailed them. He was jogging along on One-eye, or rather Buddy, as Mose called him. He beamed with delight at the sight of the two of them and began to talk. There was nothing to do but to slow down to the mule's gait and listen.

Here it was—the made-over Bailey cabin. This was the same house, built of the old hand-hewn boards and beams, yet how different it looked, sitting here on Crabapple Creek, with a new roof and a new coat of paint as white as the dogwood blooms on the hills. Something else was new—that electric meter gleaming on the side wall. But for all these changes, Granny's roses and snowball bushes seemed to belong in this spot. So did Ma Bailey in her rocking chair on the porch and Pa Bailey mending a piece of broken harness in the barn door. And wasn't that mockingbird in the lilac bush the same one which used to bubble over with song just like that in Bee Tree Hollow?

However, Cynthia was not looking at this house. She looked out through the years and saw the homeplace of her own she would have someday.

THE END

More Books from The Good and the Beautiful Library!

**Prudence Crandall:
Woman of Courage**
by Elizabeth Yates

**Harriet, The Moses of
Her People**
by Sarah H. Bradford

Black Hawk
by Arthur J. Beckhard

**Jacqueline of
the Carrier Pigeons**
by Augusta Huiell Seaman

www.thegoodandthebeautiful.com